Scags at 18

Scags at 18

Deborah Emin

New York

Copyright © 2011 by Deborah Emin

Published by Sullivan Street Press, Inc., New York

Cover and interior design by Patricia Rasch

ISBN 978-0-9819428-7-2 for print version
ISBN 978-0-9819428-9-6 for .pdf
ISBN 978-0-9819428-8-9 for .epub

With love for Suzanne Pyrch
In memory of John Stoddard

Mama handed me this diary at the train station. I don't think she realized what effect this gift would have on me. I'm sure my face betrayed how frightened I was of leaving home. She must have thought a diary would be helpful, be a companion on the train ride. When I opened her present as the train pulled out of the station, the first thing that caught my eye was my name, Scags Morgenstern, embossed on its blue leather cover.

All the way to Vermont, I clutched my new diary to my chest. I wanted to write down my impressions—what I saw out the train window or what I heard other passengers say. Not one word found its way onto this first page. My mind froze all the way from Chicago to here. My pen refused to click open. I didn't even doodle on the clean pages of this book. I sat still in my seat, eyes open but seeing nothing. Much of the Midwest and then the East clattered past my window.

It wasn't until I arrived into this new world, unlike anything I had ever seen, that my eyes and ears and nose began registering what was here. The mountains, the pine trees and green fields stunned me. This summer, as I sat at my desk at home, fantasizing about arriving here, I had no idea what this new world would be like. My fantasies were seedlings that sought a different soil from that in Skokie. I definitely wanted to plant myself in a new place. But I had no idea what this "this" was like.

In the cab ride from the train station to the campus, I began to observe the height of the mountains, the ubiquitous pine trees and their perfume which filled up the whole atmosphere. I've never smelled anything like it; it made me cry.

I can confirm that New Englanders are taciturn. The cab driver didn't say one word to me the entire time I sat in his back seat, clutching my purse, tears roaming across my cheeks as the sheer magnitude of the differences I was about to participate in struck me.

I sat staring out the window. My eyes recorded the scenery now passing by. The winding roads, the red-covered bridges, the white houses built so close to the road. Once we turned off the two-laned highway, though, I knew I had entered another kingdom, where I was about to either find myself or end up terribly lost.

The big black cab drove under a huge sign, a metal sign, with the College's name entwined in it. The sign sat balanced on two white columns on either side of the long driveway that leads up here. The ride was interminable. I thought maybe I had been tricked, that this couldn't be the way to where I was going to spend the next four years of my life. The driveway was long with these vast empty spaces of well tended lawns, clean and sprawling but seemingly leading nowhere. But in the distance, such a long distance, surely there had to be the College.

When we neared the summit, the cab pulled up to a stop near a white booth that looked like a toll booth in a fairy tale. A man in a blue uniform stepped out of it, clipboard in hand. He put his face through the lowered back window to look at me and ask my name. Thank God, he found it on his list. He checked it off and motioned for the cab driver to continue to my dorm. We continued our upward drive.

Then, there it was, spread out before me: The magic kingdom of my dreams, the place I had worked so hard to get to. In its reality, it was too fantastical for me to believe. I had never in my life seen such a place as this. It looked like a movie set.

The cab driver took my bags out of the trunk of the cab. I hadn't noticed him pulling up to my dormitory. I got out of his cab and stood still as the only person I knew so far left me. In the afternoon air filled with fall's dust, I watched the red lights of his cab disappear down the long drive. I was alone.

There was nothing left to be done standing around. I picked up my suitcase and book bag and trudged up the two flights of stairs to my room. Inside, I found my roommate, Sylvie, sitting on her bed, the one closest to the door. Her clothes sat in piles waiting for some order to be established. Sylvie barely noticed my arrival other than to tell me her name and to say hello. I think I disturbed her. She looked like she was deep in thought. Once she had put her clothes away, Sylvie hurried out the door.

If I were still the surly but sure Scags who needed to get out of Skokie as fast as possible, I might have struck up a conversation with Sylvie. I've been deserted by that Scags. I remember her sitting at my desk during the awful boredom of this past August (which was only two weeks ago). She couldn't bear watching the slow hands on the clock creeping along. She hated the hot air that suffocated us and refused to pack or even walk her dog. She sat at her desk, drawing self-portraits. She drew seedlings about to burst.

Now that I'm here—well—I'm not that surly Scags about to burst. When I introduce myself, I don't sound like me at all. I sound like Lennie in "Of Mice and Men." You know, the guy who is a bit slow and talks about liking to stroke soft things whenever people talk to him. Everyone else speaks normally, not me, not this Scags.

In my fantasy of my new life away from Skokie, I never imagined I would feel lonely.

The loneliness came crashing down on me. So, I decided to call my Pops. I wanted to hear his voice. That's what loneliness can do to me. I never seek him out. Generally, I avoid him. It isn't that I don't love him, I do, but his crazy behavior makes me feel nuts. It's as if his craziness were contagious.

I waited for the other people on my floor to leave. I was embarrassed to use the phone booth at the end of the hall. I had never called long distance before. I entered the booth and carefully read all the instructions printed on the phone. I deposited my dime, an operator came on after only two rings and I gave her all the information she asked for. Except I forgot to warn her that we were trying to call a crazy person.

How quickly I forgot how difficult it is for Pops to do new things. When the operator told him he needed to accept the charge for the call, he didn't understand why he had to accept the charge. He demanded a full explanation of where those charges would go and what would happen to him once he agreed.

Well, that's my Pops. I did hear his voice. After listening to the operator being as nice as possible to Pops, I had to speak up. I couldn't take his worrying about the phone company wanting to rip him off. I told the nice operator that I didn't want to place the call after all. I hung up the phone. I sat in the phone booth trying to get over how hard he made things. Why couldn't he just agree to pay for the call from his only daughter away at college for the first time?

I couldn't sit in the phone booth anymore. I

heard voices coming up the stairs so I ran down the two flights of stairs and outside into the most beautiful day I have ever seen. Life was everywhere. My fellow students looked like a bumper crop of dandelions. Bright and fresh and strong, they took over the lawns and the roadways, even the parking lots filled with their riotous growth. The raucous sounds of them yelling hello, grabbing onto their old friends, welcoming everyone back made me see what I had been longing for. I watched for a few moments and then headed for the nearest path away from their collective happiness.

I wanted to run away from it all but I don't know my way around. I followed the path I was on. The sounds on campus faded behind me. I walked and walked until the path ended and I found myself in an orchard. No one was there.

I stood on the perimeter of the orchard and stared into it, noticing an orchard for the first time. I have read about orchards and eaten my fill of apples, but I have never been in one.

I had no idea what an orchard's life was like. I stepped from the path and walked straight into it, following no particular path, as there was none. Everything that happened was brand new to me. Apples fell to the earth and burst open. Bees working sounded like saws sawing on wood. They were everywhere but didn't frighten me. They paid no attention to me; they had so much work to do. The sun was warm but not hot.

I began pulling apples from the trees. I wanted to see what they tasted like direct from tree to me. I put one in the palm of my hand. It looked like a small globe with red masses and green masses.

I stared at it for a long time before biting into it. The colors could have been painted on. I was in awe of myself. Here I was standing in an orchard so far from home with this amazing apple in my hand.

When I bit into it, as my teeth pierced the skin, I was aware of every single sensation—of the sweet juices shooting out from between my lips and down my chin and then along my arm. The stickiness attracted the bees. The bees swarmed around me, humming over my head.

I didn't care. I ate as many apples as I wanted to and dropped their cores to the ground. The abundance in the orchard made me feel wealthy. For a moment, I wasn't lost. I said out loud for the bees and the trees to hear, "Home wasn't built in a day." That made me laugh.

I laughed myself silly. I ate apples until I couldn't fit another inside my stomach.

Then I realized I didn't know how to get back to the campus. I had turned myself every which way so I could taste as many different apples as possible from as many different trees. In the process of filling myself up, I had gotten myself lost, again.

My rescue came unexpectedly within minutes. I heard The Beatles song, "Lucy in the Sky with Diamonds" come swooshing into the orchard from the open dorm windows. The exuberant music became my bread crumbs, leading me back out of the orchard and onto the path that leads back here.

I was so relieved by my good fortune, I hurried along, not wanting to lose my way back before the song ended. In my haste, I didn't pay attention to anything but following that music. No surprise then when I walked right into a man racing along the path. He swerved to get past me and fell down a small incline, sending gravel, leaves and his shoe into the air.

I offered him my hand to help pull him out of the little ravine he had fallen into but he popped up from it, laughing. I couldn't believe it.

"I'm okay," he said, touching his arms, his legs, his back, checking to see if indeed he was okay. "Yep, I'm fine. Really." He laughed all the time, and hopped around trying to put his shoe back on and tie it.

"That's good," I said. I didn't know what else to say.

I noticed, however, that my breadcrumb song had ended. I waited to see if this man I had almost injured would be able to get me back where I needed to go. I couldn't ask him. I was afraid of how he might look at me.

Turns out he is more polite than I am and even introduced himself to me as the cross country coach. His name is Alex. He made it clear to me that there were two teams, one for the men and one for the women.

"I didn't know there were women's teams," I said. I looked at him to see if he cared what I was about to say, "I trained with the boys team in high school, but I never competed."

It felt like I was showing off. I don't usually talk about running. No one at home seemed interested that I ran with the boys. Alex, though, was most impressed.

I guess it is impressive that I could keep up with them. I never thought about it. I like running. I like it so much I was willing to be with them as they charged along the paths, spitting and swearing and pushing each other out of the way. They ignored me. But I could keep up with them.

Alex suddenly asked me to try out for the team.

I didn't expect that. "I need to think about it," I said, "my classes have to come first."

"Of course," he said, "but you should try competing. It changes everything."

By then we had reached a spot where I knew where I was. In my eagerness to get back up to my dorm room, I walked away from Alex. But Alex didn't let me walk off like that. He came after me and tapped me on the shoulder.

"I've told you my name, but what's yours?"

I said, "Scags Morgenstern."

He looked me right in the eye and said, "Okay, Scags. We have a practice tomorrow morning. Meet us at 7:00 in the courtyard of the phys ed building." With that, he walked away.

I didn't have a chance to say yes or no. I lingered for a moment, watching him run back the way we had come. For the first time, I tried to imagine what it would be like to actually win a race rather than just pretending to myself that I could win one, given the chance.

With all of these new thoughts racing around inside me, I made myself come back up to my room so I could write down all this great new stuff that is happening to me. Maybe this gift from Mama will be useful after all.

I'm never going to have any friends here. I've tried but it's useless. They ask me, "What's your name?"

I answer, "Scags."

They ask me, "What's a Scags?"

Or they ask me where I am from. I answer, "Skokie."

They ask me, "What's a Skokie?"

That was how things ended this morning when I joined Alex and the "teams" for the morning run. The run was great. I loved it. Early mornings here are so different from in Skokie. When we went running there, it was flat for one thing. Here, the terrain varies and the muscles in my legs got a work out they've never had before. At some points, I couldn't keep up.

When we finished, I was so tired, I had to sit for a while to cool down and that was when the questions began. "What's a Scags?" "What's a Skokie?"

I've always been proud of my name. I know I hated Skokie but now I hate it more.

Okay, everyone has to be from somewhere. Sylvie, my roommate, is from Montreal. No one asks her what that is. They know what it is.

Why does anyone care where I'm from? Why when I say I'm from Skokie do they look at me as if I said I was from Mars? Being from Mars would make me interesting to them. They can't understand that a person can be from nowhere interesting but still be an interesting person. What's wrong with them?

Oh well, after the run, I had my 10:30 appointment with my advisor. I got so worked up about setting up my schedule that I almost left the dorm room wearing a sneaker and a sandal. Sylive saved me. As I walked out the door, she asked me: "Hey Scags, is that the best footwear you can find? It's a charming pair but not too practical." I thanked her profusely as I exchanged my sneaker for a sandal and then ran to my appointment.

Prof. Keating's office is in the Humanities Building. A big, red-painted, two-story wooden building shaped like a U, it's close to the dorm. His office/classroom is on the second floor. I trudged up the wooden staircase and found his office right away. I started to walk in the door but he was talking to another student. I didn't know how long I would have to wait, so I plopped myself down on a bench at the end of the hall. As soon as I sat down, the other student left.

Prof. Keating's head appeared from his doorway. He peered one way and then the other, like a periscope on a submarine, until he spied me and motioned for me to come in. He has white hair even though he seems to be pretty young. I have never seen a young person with old peoples' hair. The skin on his face has a gleaming rubbed-red-by-life look to it. Probably that is due to his motorcycling. In his faded and torn blue jeans, blue jeans shirt and motorcycle boots, he wasn't what I expected at all.

His whole attitude was contrary to the motorcycle look. He's all about getting things done, moving along, not relishing anything—not the fact that I had never been to college before or how hard I worked to get here.

No, he rushed me through everything.

I wanted to talk to him about so many things. Not just the important decisions about my first semester which were of course the most important things we should have talked about. I wanted to talk about things like which professors were best for me to know and why. How should I balance my required courses against the ones I choose for my own edification? How was I to plan for the next semester?

I had only sat down in this very comfortable chair next to his desk when he buried his head in a gridsheet spread across his desk. I noticed him putting my initials into little squares. I realized he was making all my decisions for me. I tried to interrupt him but he didn't hear me.

I know I got angry. My whole face and neck turn red when I am upset. I mean, I hadn't even had the necessary time to explain to him who I am. He handed me a sheet of paper with my schedule on it. He looked at me as if I should know to leave.

Then as I stomped out the door, he called me back. I thought he was going to change his mind about my schedule and we would go over it again, give it more careful attention.

He looked at me for a long while, then shook his head and said, "I had a note from Mr. Schoors about you. Seems he wants you on the women's cross country team. I told him I would make sure your schedule could accommodate that. That's what your Phys. Ed. class is. Good luck."

I had forgotten about running. I had no idea who Mr. Schoors was but then remembered Alex. Everyone has a last name, I just didn't know his.

Then Prof. Keating dismissed me. "That's all for now, Scags. See you around." His eyes followed me out the door.

Every day fills up with something new. Thank God is all I can say. Yesterday was one set of events and today was a completely different one. A far, far better set. Maybe I am now on the upswing. Because today was the day that I met my first friend and went to a poetry reading. Life here is so full of surprises.

I woke up in such a bad mood. I hated that meeting with Prof. Keating. Come on, I wanted to go screaming back at him, this is the best you can do for me? This is my schedule for my first semester?

I couldn't calm down. I went for breakfast and listened to more kids telling each other how much they missed each other over the summer. I can't escape being the new kid, can I?

I walked towards the new arts building after breakfast. Well, I really followed some students headed in that direction. They walked fast and disappeared into the building before I had a chance to realize where I was.

It isn't every day that I make a new friend. In Skokie, that never happened. The friends you had were the friends you had. Who we grew up with, that was who we knew. For better or worse, I should add.

When the students I followed went through the large main door, I couldn't see where they had gone and panicked. I ran after them, burst open the door and bam—I did it again—I ran right into someone and knocked the door right into her.

I had opened the door too fast as she was trying to open it from the other side. She had her hand held out and the door really hit it. She might have gotten really angry at me and walked away.

Instead, she saw my red face and neck and arms and took pity on me.

"You're new," she said. And then she laughed too. Just like Alex had laughed.

"Yes," I said, "It is becoming all too obvious that I don't know my way around here. I keep getting lost and then knocking into someone."

She looked at me for a couple of seconds and then said, "My name is Eileen."

"Scags," I said.

She took my arm and turned me around and we walked out of the arts building.

"I need a cup of coffee. Come with me."

That was all it took for us to become friends. My first official friend. Eileen is from Brooklyn, like Mr. Arthur, Julia's father. I love it that she has a small connection to my other life. She too is a scholarship student, like me.

"We're the poor people here. Everyone else lives on a trust fund but not us. We live off our scholarships. Must mean we're a lot smarter than they are. Right?"

She said all of that with such a devilish look

in her eyes. She is a singer. She writes her own songs. She has her whole life laid out. Study music here. Go back to New York and become a star. She has that look about her. I can see it. She will do exactly as she says. It was thrilling to listen to her talk about her plans.

When she asked me what I wanted to study, I said, "Everything. I don't know yet what it is I really want to do. I just want to be a student until I figure out my life. I'm good at being a student."

When we couldn't drink any more coffee without exploding, we left the Commons and ended up at my now new favorite place—the orchard. Now it is our orchard and not just mine. We walked arm in arm along the same path I had been on yesterday in my blue lonely mood. What a difference having a friend makes.

Eileen sang to me as we walked. I remember Odessa and Pops singing to me when I was a little kid. Eileen singing her new song to me was different. This is more of what I wanted when I was fantasizing about my new life. Having a friend who has new things to teach me.

Eileen's song isn't finished yet. She told me she wanted it to be so much more than it is now. I like it, I kept telling her. She kept trying to find the right words to tell the story of a young girl, sitting on her fire escape, singing to her imaginary friend, Mr. Lucky. She asks him to help her find a boyfriend to take her away from her stifling life at home. All the words to the song aren't written yet but the tune was mournful and hopeful at the same time. I could definitely feel what she wanted to say. I told her that. She almost cried she was so happy that I liked her song.

I could have cried too. Not only was the song beautiful and her voice too, but I know that feeling—that longing. I remember lying in bed, wishing, no, really, bargaining with God to not just get me away from home but to help me find someone to really love me. I don't want to write about this now.

Now that I'm back here in my room, I want to put down my thoughts about Eileen. It's clear that we're not at all alike. She's not as tall as me or the same age as me. She wears lots of makeup, or a lot in comparison to me who wears none.

To be fair, I guess as a performer, she has to wear makeup. Her hair is black, and I mean dark shiny black. It fits her head like a helmet. It's even thicker than mine. Out doors, not one hair on her head moved. My hair is red.

She's heavy too. I know that makes me sound like a terrible person, but I don't mean to be mean but she could lose some weight. Maybe the size of a singer matters and she needs that larger body for the music, but I do think she would be happier to be slimmer. I don't know, it's in the way she carries herself that makes me think she isn't that comfortable inside her own skin. She wore pretty clothes, in lots of colors that I can never wear due to my hair color. So, I guess, all in all, we aren't the same physically but I don't think that will make a difference at all when it comes to being friends.

Because ultimately, it must be about who we are and what we share about our lives that makes a good friend. I admire Eileen for knowing that she will be a singer/songwriter. How wonderful. She is exactly how I would describe a performer—ready to react to anything that happens and to be able to express in her being how that makes her feel.

My Aunt Money would call her dramatic. I think of her as having those performer qualities that include bigger than normal gestures and a louder than normal voice.

When we were in the orchard, we ate a couple of apples and then she had to leave. She was off to a lesson. She's lucky, not only does she know what she wants to do with her life, but her work has begun. When she left, I felt like my world got empty again.

Then she came back into my world again without any warning. Around 6:30 she came bursting into my room. From the look on her face, I thought something had happened. No, silly me, it was about to happen.

She came into my room and without saying much, took me by the hand and pulled me out the door. I had been at my desk, reading a letter from Goldie. In the envelope was a $20 bill. Goldie wrote she would send me one of those every month. I felt rich and lucky and then Eileen's appearance proved I was correct.

She dragged me out the door and down the stairs. I stuffed the letter and money into my pocket and kept up with Eileen wondering what the hurry was all about. Turns out we were racing to a poetry reading.

I'd never been to one before. Following Eileen on the dark path back to the arts building, my ears rang with the news that life was now very different. I had a friend who rushed me off to a poetry reading at night. There was no one I had to ask permission of to leave the dorm or to race like that in the dark. It was truly unreal to me.

I'd never heard of the poet, but now that I've heard him in person, I want to read everything he's written. Why didn't I know who Robert Lowell is?

He walked onto the stage and the audience cheered. I didn't know that poets got cheered like that.

We sat in the front row because all the other seats were taken by the time we got to the theater. I could hear the pages of his book turn as he read.

He stood close to me. I heard his voice and the way he cleared his throat—we could have been alone in a room together. He performed for me alone. It was like the entire time he stood on the stage, he was leading me to a very specific point, intended just for me.

He read a poem called "Skunk Hour." When he came to this one line in the poem

"My mind's not right"

I knew he read that poem just for me. At that moment, the words came soaring through the air like an arrow shot out to hit its truest mark and that was me. It hit me and I was stunned out of the old Scags and ushered into this new Scags. I could have dropped dead at that moment and my life was complete. I had no idea poetry could sting like that.

I couldn't tell Eileen or anyone what had happened to me. I would have had to explain too many other things. How necessary is it really to let people know about my past? Isn't it enough that I am here now and quickly not being that old Scags but this newer one? The one now stung by that arrow sent for me to push me out of that old hole I sat in and into this new place where every day was like a huge fireworks display in my head.

I wanted to spend time with Mr. Lowell alone. Now that wasn't possible. There were so many people hanging around him once the reading was over. I learned, though, just as I think Eileen looks like a performer, Mr. Lowell is a poet to me. A poet should look like he can never find his car keys but that he's really looking for something much more important. A poet's eyes should be shifty. He has to be trying to see things no one else can see and we are just getting in his way. At least that is what Mr. Lowell looked like to me.

When I asked Eileen why they all cheered when Mr. Lowell walked onto the stage, she told me that he was in Chicago last summer for the Democratic Convention. I could have seen him, I thought, but no, not me, I was too busy writing my college essays to go downtown for the convention protests. But he was there with all these other cool people. I didn't know anything about it and I was right there.

Eileen also told me that he had been a conscientious objector during the Second World War and gone to prison for it. That blew my mind. I mean I don't think about war that much. Maybe I should. Would I go to prison to avoid a war because I believed it was wrong? These questions aren't on any recent tests I've taken but they should have been.

As Eileen and I walked around the campus together after the reading, I still felt stung by his poems. I was troubled by how he could balance writing such personal poetry and be so involved in the anti-war protests. He has been working for a presidential candidate as well, Eugene McCarthy. Turns out he's a poet too. Do we really have poets running for president now? Since when?

We stomped all over the campus together for what seemed like hours. Eileen talked about how she had gone to anti-war protests and written songs about it. I listened. There was nothing for me to say.

Eileen had lots of things to say about why this war was wrong. I don't know yet. I haven't given it any thought and for the first time it has occurred to me that I should be thinking about things like this.

"Always better to be silent when you know nothing about a topic," Goldie says. Now, though, there are too many things I need to know that my silence won't help me to learn.

I asked Eileen what she thought about the war and she began to tell me things I never really had heard before. Pops turning on the news at home had meant only one thing to me— I was free to go to my room and study. It was as if while Pops watched the news, I could be released from needing to be worried about him. He focused on the bums in office and the bums on the sports fields. I went to my room to study so I could get a scholarship and get as far away as possible from all of that. While he worried about politics and sports,

I worked my way here. I got away from him and Skokie. Then I arrived here and discovered how involved everyone is in what happens in the world. I'm glad I heard Mr. Lowell read but I have so much work to do now.

I'm ready for classes to start tomorrow. My clothes are in order for the entire week. I've become friends with the library.

This morning, I got to breakfast in the Commons late. Eileen appeared. She sat down at my table as if she always had breakfast with me. I ate my bowl of oatmeal and fruit. Eileen sat down to a breakfast of bagel with cream cheese, coffee cake, juice and coffee. I was too nervous to eat like that.

She was going to practice for the whole day, of course. I like how when she says to me, "I need to hurry and get to the practice room," how I feel so much a part of her life now.

Eileen asked me what I was doing today. I told her I was going to the library to study it more closely.

"Scags, you are great. I don't know anyone who goes to a library to study it. I love you."

She just says things like that and I don't ever know what to say back.

I went into this long explanation about my existential need for libraries but I could see she lost interest quickly.

Who needs to listen to me go on and on about the function of a library? I know in my heart of hearts that Eileen and I are different in many ways. Even though we are both here on scholarship, I am the one who is the student and she is the one who is the musician. There's a huge difference between the two, believe me.

Books breathe and live in libraries and wait for us to take them from the shelves and drink from them. Like little springs that bubble up out of the strangest places, they open up to reveal secret worlds. And each book has his or her own opinion about everything. They argue constantly about the meaning, the beauty and the sense of life. I wanted to share these thoughts with Eileen but she wanted to practice.

I sound like I'm on a mission to change the way people think about libraries. I get carried away and go on and on about how libraries should be the center of our lives. No one has ever agreed with me.

Eileen left and I went to introduce myself to the library. I spent hours there. By the time I left, the sun had set. During the day, the library looks as if it is feeding off the side of the mountain. At night, with the lights on, it glows like a hovering hive. When the lights go off, the whole building disappears, as if it doesn't exist.

Its architectural design is distinctly different from the rest of this place. The College qualifies as a movie set for "quaint and monied." I admit I like that look. Eileen calls the campus look, "New England charming." She thinks the library's steel and glass exterior was someone's bad idea stuck in a spot on the side of the mountain not many people see.

The interior though makes one forget the exterior. The moment I entered, it sucked me in and delivered me into this extremely rich environment. Yes. It was designed for those who love libraries. No, that's not giving it its due. This library was specifically conceived and created for people like me.

I know how self-centered that sounds. But it was.

First of all, you can't believe the size of its collection. It's immense. This is the Arts and Humanities Library. There is a small Science collection housed here but the larger one is in the Science building across campus. I saw a sign saying that the majority of the Social Sciences collection is in another building as well.

Let me begin at the moment I walked through the doors. I walked into this dark area where the reference desk, sign out desks and reserve desk all were. Quiet reigned as it should in a library. As I walked in from the bright outdoors to the cool, dark and silent inside, the main floor made it clear already that a master of the library had put this all together. There are two more floors above this entryway. Each has windows on three sides. On each of those floors, he wall where the library sits parked into the side of the mountain is interesting too. They have a small cafe on each floor, restrooms and phone booths. I could live in the library.

The reading rooms were furnished with an abundance of long wooden tables. Row upon row of dark tables filled the rooms. Beyond the tables and along the northern wall, armchairs nestled in little groups with ottomans and side tables arranged to make those areas as comfortable as possible. All the available floor space was carpeted to cut down on the noise so you walked on these plush woven fabrics in various shades of green.

I had to sit in every chair and run my hands along the tables feeling their smooth finish. Then I walked over to the windows and looked outside from each vantage point. No matter which way I looked, I saw trees. We were up in the trees like squirrels in our nests.

I sat down at one of the long tables closest to a window facing west and watched the sky changing. It never stopped changing. The clouds came through quickly, always in a rush; their sizes and colors whirling through as if they had no time to stop.

With the amount of sunlight that came through the window today, I saw how easy it will be to use my sun clock approach to studying here too. The long tables are perfect for laying out my books and papers and for also watching the the progress of the sun as the day goes by. I prefer that way to tell time to any other when I work in the library.

My classes may begin now. I am ready for the

long days of my "P" schedule as Eileen called it. My Pottery, Philosophy, Psychology, Poetry and Phys. Ed classes are about to start. I've set my alarm for 5:30.

I'm glad I had all that time to wander through the entire library. If Sylvie were in our room now, I could share with her the secrets I learned. She's quite popular already. So, she's out with her friends. People come and go here with such ease. They have cars. Did I write here yet that my next door neighbor, Kit, has a Bentley and drives it to the Commons for breakfast?

I'm ready for tomorrow and even though it is only 9:30, it never hurts to get a good night's sleep. I have a team run in the morning before my classes start. Did I say I was excited? And nervous? I wish Mama and Pops were here to wish me well.

My first day of classes got off to a rocky start.

Here I am sitting in my dorm room again. I could see people hooking up for coffee after classes. They went to the Commons and the noise was so loud that I had to come back up here. Sylvie must think I never leave the room.

This first day threw me that's for sure. Well, it was really just one class that made me feel this way. When you know, as I do, that you're the pet project of a couple of your high school teachers and if they saw what happened today they would wonder why they poured all their energy into you, well...

I'm really not angry. Nor am I ungrateful. I know it took my hard work too to get me into this place. The two of them played a significant role in helping me. I feel like I am now on the road to disappointing them.

I sat through this first day of classes and wondered what Miss Fromm and Mrs. Wald were thinking of. What would they do if they were me?

My assessment is this: When it comes to purely academic classes like the psychology and philosophy classes, I am a whiz kid. My two other classes aren't as certain when it comes to my abilities as a student. Or, in the case of Dr. Fish's poetry class, my perceived abilities. Or my innate inabilities due to my feminine nature.

Mrs. Wald might know what to say to someone

like Dr. Fish, but she isn't here. Both of them were great when it came to coaching me for the interview. We sat for hours and we had a good time doing it. They asked serious questions but then they would ask just plain silly ones to help me relax and enjoy myself.

Dr. Fish would never understand that kind of student/teacher relationship because he is aptly named Dr. Fish. Or as I am now dubbing him—old fuck face. Yes, I can be like this here in my room and in my diary, but in person, he is as awful as his name sounds.

It could not have been a worse start to our class than for him to say, as he did, that no woman, not one, is capable of writing or understanding poetry. I am not making this up. I heard him say those very words. He intimidated me, the way he stood in front of the class and counted the number of women sitting there. It was like he couldn't stand the fact of us being there.

When I learned how to dissect a fish in Miss Fromm's biology class, I never knew that I might be fantasizing doing it on a human.

The nagging question in the back of my head is this: What if he fails me and I lose my scholarship?

I could barely put those words on this page. Nor can I keep up this attitude of being so smart and it will all turn out to be okay.

I returned from classes and went to the bathroom and threw up right away. I didn't care who was in there, I had no time to care.

As I recovered from throwing up, I imagined two options. The first was I could run away. The second is I could pretend to be someone else. I'd still have to be a girl but maybe if I weren't me who was so scared, I'd do okay.

Why do they let him teach here?

Okay, Scags, you've got to stop this complaining because then there is the other class you know you will have trouble with but for other reasons.

In the pottery class that Prof. Keating insisted I take, I am up against something else I'm not sure of. I wanted to be in an art history class, but no, he placed me in a studio arts class. I'm not an artist. I don't know anything about throwing pots, I didn't even know that was what one did or called it. At least Prof. Calderon is a nicer person and so much better to look at than Dr. Fish.

I can only tackle one big problem at a time. Prof. Calderon may be easier to talk to than Dr. Fish will ever be. I felt so out of place there. It was more than just the content of the class—the throwing pots—it had to do with the way she walked around the class talking to us. So personal in a way I have never seen before. I didn't know how to respond to it at all.

After dinner, I'll go to the library. At least there

I know what to do and feel competent. I think I should wait until the end of the week to run away. Maybe by then I will have calmed down.

I couldn't stay away from this diary. Something else unexpected and unplanned for occurred today and I wanted to write about it.

When I went to breakfast this morning, I found a note in my mailbox from Prof. Keating. He apologized for the late notice but this was an invitation to a small gathering at his house of new and returning students. He promised we would have a good time and that he wouldn't keep us too late.

I was torn. I wanted to go to his house and see what it was like but I had planned to be in the library all evening. It's a good thing that Goldie's sayings keep popping into my head. Her suggestion for this evening was—plans are meant to be changed. So, I dutifully walked to Prof. Keating's house guided by the map he enclosed with his invitation. Fortunately, there's a lit path that goes directly from the campus to faculty housing and his house is at the end of it. No mistaking which house is his.

I arrived a little early and a lot nervous. I rang the bell and entered through a large wooden front door into a large front hallway that was filled with the clutter of his family's life. I smelled their dinner when the door flew open, held onto by his son who looks exactly like him but much younger. He silently led me to their library.

I walked into that room and was all alone.

Photos of family and friends sat on the book-shelves making it impossible to read the titles of the books. Instead of trying to read the titles by removing the pictures, I sat down on a long, leather couch and picked up some literary journals lying about. His son left too fast for me to say one word. He has the same hair color and skin color as his father, though—white hair and red skin.

I heard Mrs. Keating's voice in another room. Her laughter rang throughout the house and set the glassware chattering in response to her bray-ing. I wish I knew what she had been laughing at.

Prof. Keating came into the library carry-ing a large tray with bottles of pop as well as a large bottle of red wine. He set it down on a glass-covered table right in front of me and then disappeared. He returned quickly, with another tray filled with cheese, crackers and cookies. Out he went again for the glasses and by then the room began to fill up with other students, thank God.

Prof. Keating wasn't really comfortable with us in his home. There were 13 of us. I recognized two guys from my philosophy class and a woman from the pottery class, or the pot throw, as I call it. Everyone else was a complete stranger. How does a school this small have so many unknown people in it?

I said one word to one person I didn't know. I said "hi" to a guy named Charles. Prof. Keating didn't seem to like Charles very much which seemed odd to me.

Charles intrigued me, though. Of all the people I've met so far, he strikes me as the most interesting. It's like he's in a movie as he moves through life. He wears a leather jacket, slicks his hair away from his face so you can see exactly what he is thinking or feeling. It is written there for all to see. Most of the other guys have very long hair that obscures their faces. Charles chewed on a match stick and the harder he chewed, the more intense his thoughts seemed to be. Out of his jacket pocket a long-titled book by Tom Wolfe poked out. The book was thin but the title was endless.

He sat hunched over the glass table at Prof. Keating's house, chewing on the matchstick and patiently listening but with a bored look on his face. Since I felt as invisible as I usually do, I watched him and hoped he didn't notice that. Everyone else became more animated and as they ate the food and drank the wine, their voices rose and they all seemed to feel at home. When the food and wine were gone, like a silent agreement, they left.

I'm not sure why we were there. I heard Prof. Keating say he would be doing this regularly throughout the term.

I watched Charles for the entire time we sat there. He remained still and minded his own business. He didn't speak up or to anyone. Some students knew him and said hello. He nodded at them. It was when I saw his smile and big blue eyes shine out of his face that something inside of me went kerplunk. You know, something happened and for one moment he looked at me that way too. He looked at me and I knew he saw me. I couldn't turn away, I wanted to, but I was frozen in place.

When everyone got up to leave, Charles disappeared out the door. Prof. Keating unexpectedly grabbed my hand and asked me to stay a bit longer. I wanted to get out the door. I had spent the whole day in classes and didn't want to talk or have to listen to anyone.

He invited me to stay for dinner. I was hungry and the idea of a home cooked meal was very tempting and it was such a good thing I stayed. The food was delicious. It was a feast.

Mrs. Keating was in the kitchen. Large and dark and loud, she wasn't at all like her husband or their two kids. She was very nice and sweet to me. She asked me questions about what my life was like before I got to the College. She had some disparaging words about this place but said them in such a funny way, I thought, she doesn't mean them. I liked sitting at their table, the four Keatings and me. Mrs. Keating had such big hands and such a wide mouth that she looked more like a farm worker than a professor's wife. Her kids seemed embarrassed by her, she could talk kind of rough as if she were a farmer. She called the other professors and their wives "uptight asswipes."

By the time we finished dinner, I was filled up and bit drunk. Mrs. Keating disappeared from the kitchen and the two kids ran up to their rooms to do their homework. Prof. Keating walked me back here.

The kids are wonderful. I would be their friend if their father weren't my advisor. I know that. They are twins. Her name is Robin and he is named Jeffrey. They look like Prof. Keating. Mrs. Keating is large and I mean large but in her manner as well as her appearance.

Prof. Keating walked with me, he said, because he needed air after all that food and wine. I was glad for his company. We walked slowly and watched the stars in the sky. The sky was clear and up here in the mountains, it's possible to feel much closer to the stars than we are.

"I'm waiting for the harvest moon to rise," I told Prof. Keating.

He asked me why and I told him the story of how my family had made that night a family holiday.

"The story goes like this," I said to him. We stopped along the path and sat down on a bench.

"When I was a little kid, my parents and I were out for a walk at night. We had gone to a movie at my school and wandered home. All of a sudden I noticed the moon rising and it was so big I burst out crying. My Pops had to pick me up. I had become too frightened to walk any further.

"They might have laughed at me but they didn't. They understood how that outsized moon could be so startling to a little kid. So, we had a ritual every fall after that. As soon as we knew the Harvest Moon was going to rise, we would go outside. Pops would put me on his shoulders until I got too big for that and we would watch the moon rise and tell stories about her size, her color and why she was the way she was. The trick was to change the story every year. Otherwise, we would be creating a fetish, my Pops said. We needed to keep it fresh."

Prof. Keating sat in silence as I told my story. At the end of it, he turned to me and said that the College had made a wise choice in selecting me to come on scholarship.

"I like the fact that you come from an imaginative family that values creativity."

There was something about the way he said it that sounded better than it does on the page. He was sincere and it felt different from how I had experienced him in his office or even over dinner when he barely lifted his face from his plate.

I tried to find a way to ask him about Charles but I could sense that this wasn't the best time. We were both so tired. I left him downstairs at the doorway and came back up to my room to write in here. Somehow these new experiences are more real to me once I enter them in my diary.

Charles intrigues me. He isn't a Chuck or a Charlie. Charles. He doesn't know that I am interested in him or that I have been following him around. That is when I'm not studying. Oh you of little faith, of course I am not wasting my time mooning over some guy as Goldie warned me not to do. Her big fear was that away from home, I would lose direction and forget why I had won this scholarship. Of course not. I'm just intrigued by him and want to learn more about him.

When he came to the library today, he picked up a large stack of newspapers and magazines and sat down in an easy chair not far from where I was working. How convenient I thought. From time to time, I felt his eyes on me and so I turned slowly, as if just pausing in thought, to see if he was looking at me. He was. He recognized me, I'm sure. He smiled. One thing I noticed about him was how methodically he read his papers. He placed the ones to be read at his left foot and went through it from front to back, folded it neatly and set it down next to his right foot.

When he walked by my spot at the table, I smelled him and it was a mixture of cigarettes and coffee, not unlike my Pops with his cigars and coffee. Charles is about the same height as Pops. He's younger, of course, has more hair. His beautiful blue eyes shine out of him and in combination with his sunken cheeks, he almost looks like a movie star. He never takes off his leather jacket. He looks very handsome in it.

I've never used that word before—handsome—to describe someone I know. But it fits Charles. He laughs quietly and whispers to himself about the things he reads in the papers. I heard him swearing at the news, or saying, "fuck no," often. Sometimes, he threw down the papers and walked away as if they had personally insulted him. But he returned, picked up the papers and returned to his orderly reading.

I worry about him. I do. I may not know him yet but it isn't good for a person to walk around feeling upset about things in the newspapers.

Tonight before I left the library, I went to the big unabridged Websters to look up handsome. I was curious.

When I look up a word in the dictionary it is an expedition, I wanted to say to Eileen. Just as I had explained to her my love of libraries, I wanted her to hear about my love of dictionaries. Lately though with classes and her new friend, Philip, I am more alone again.

I wanted to explain to her how I feel like an explorer when I am in the dictionary. Willing to go anywhere the word takes me and to investigate whatever else may be lurking nearby to help me understand more of the world.

The word "handsome" fits Charles. As the

dictionary defined it: He is "well proportioned" and does "have a generous and gracious nature." While those qualities aren't exactly the ones I like about him, they are true as far as they go. At this moment, since I know so little about him, this word is sufficient. But I want to know more and to find better, more insightful words to describe him.

In my search for an understanding of the word "handsome" I found a term for deer grass—Handsome Harry.

Too bad his name isn't Harry. Though Charles is a perfect name for him. Charles. Not Charlie or Chuck. Charles. Good night Charles.

Following Charles around campus has some benefits. I am becoming more familiar with places, and thus feel more at ease in them. I may walk into the bookstore alone but I'm doing more than just buying a book, I'm watching to see what Charles is up to. My two days of undercover work have revealed that the Commons has a back room where there is a television, a pool table and vending machines.

I haven't seen a female friend at all. He has a buddy named Tony. They spend time together whenever Charles is on campus.

Many students know Charles. They give him big hugs and tell him how glad they are to see him back. I wonder where he was. He pats them on the shoulder, kids around with them and then he leaves with Tony. He has an old beat up Jeep that he parks near the guard station. Does he think someone will steal it? It is old and rusty and an eyesore as my Pops would say. He has New York license plates and they say, "Black Beauty." Why? I have no idea.

In my sleuthing, I heard him mention to Tony that they would be seeing "The Third Man" on Friday night.

I planned to go to the library Friday night and begin a long weekend of studying. In light of these new developments however, I plan to go to the movie as well.

I saw a poster in the Commons for the film

series on Friday nights. I'll have to go early because I am sure it will be packed. I mean, free movies. It'd be stupid and a waste not to go. Of course I will be there. I just need to plan for this and at the same time make it look really spontaneous. No one ever said that growing up was easy but this wasn't ever mentioned to me before—the ways in which to meet and get to know a guy. I'm willing to learn. Practice is a good thing. If this doesn't work out, well, there are lots of other guys here. It's just that he's so good looking.

This was the day. I woke up ready to go to the movies and to figure out how to get to know Charles better. While I had begun preparations for this new assignment, certain unforeseen events interfered with my ability to put my plans into effect.

For one thing, Dr. Fish, old fuck face, is still at it. I gave him this whole week to improve and he didn't. Today in class, I wanted desperately to answer a question. Of course, I knew the answer and of course I could have said it more eloquently than the fellow Dr. Fish called on. But I didn't get a chance. He doesn't allow women to speak. I don't know why I let him upset me but he does. As I raced out of his class, I burst into tears. Mostly out of frustration, I think. There I was in the hallway in tears when Eileen showed up. It was as if she heard me crying and came to my rescue. She saw the tears on my cheeks, took me by the arm and walked me to the orchard.

Thank God for Eileen. She apologized for not warning me about Dr. Fish. I wanted her to tell me that she had taken his class and done well. But she hadn't done well and so withdrew rather than fail it. She confirmed my worst fears. He truly hates women.

When we arrived in the orchard, my tears were gone. I enjoy spending time with her. Eileen told me about how her new relationship, that's what she called it, with Philip. They're going on a date soon. She hopes. She pulled a joint out of her pocket, lit it and passed it to me.

I must have looked like the biggest dummy on campus because I didn't know what to do. I don't smoke, anything. Pot was just a word to me and not an actual drug. Now my mind was being altered a tiny bit by the drug and it went racing around the orchard like it had been given some jet fuel to speed things up. In this altered state, I saw Eileen going off to spend time with Philip, meaning I would be alone again. I saw my worries about old fuck face being chased by my fear of failing his class and losing my scholarship. Every thought had velocity and it couldn't stop long enough for me to talk about it. That's what the pot did to me.

Eileen spoke up then and said, "Look, I can give you two pieces of advice."

She took the joint back and began a long pull on it.

"No one ever fails here unless they really mess up. He can't do a thing to you. That's what makes him so crazy. He would fail all the women but he can't. He won't fail you. Show up to class, do the work and you will pass."

"But you dropped out because he was going to fail you."

I must have looked really frightened by the prospect of failure because she told me a secret.

"I didn't work at all in his class. I couldn't take him but what they were talking about was way over my head. It wasn't for me, his class. But you'll be fine."

I didn't believe her. I wanted to though because it would have quieted down my anxiety. I was going to wait until we weren't stoned and ask her again about his class and the fact that she might have failed it.

"What's the second piece of advice?"

"When I described Dr. Fish to my mother, she told me to read Virginia Woolf's 'A Room of One's Own.' I did and while it helped me understand what male prerogatives are like and how damaging they are, I couldn't finish Dr. Fish's class but that was me."

Eileen doesn't know me well enough yet to realize how useful her advice was. No, that isn't correct. It was the best possible advice she could have given me—go read a book. The best answer to any problem in the world. How did she know that?

Still all fueled up by the pot I'd smoked, I told her I had to go. She looked puzzled but I couldn't stay there with her. I had to go to the library and find that book.

Eileen's advice got me so involved in the library that I almost forgot to go to the movies tonight. That was when the most magical series of events began. Thus the pendulum from this week began to swing in a marvelous new direction.

I was racing toward the library when I saw Charles drive up. He parked right where he always does beside the guard station. Only at that moment did I slap my head and realize I had almost forgotten about the movie. But I needed that Virginia Woolf book. I dashed off to the library, checking the time on my watch. By my calculation, I had plenty of time to find the book, check it out, go to dinner and freshen up and then stroll into the movie and find a seat near Charles. After all, that was my plan and I had prepared myself for how to approach him and what to say.

But my plans got all messed up due to the books, yes, plural, I found in the library. Purely by chance as I entered the main floor of the library and turned my head towards the reserve shelves, a title and a name caught my eye totally by surprise.

No librarians were at any of the desks. I walked straight toward that book on the reserve shelf and took the book, put it under my sweater. I know. I am becoming someone else. Who is this Scags? Well, wait, it gets worse.

In my defense, the book I spied was Dr. Fish's first book of poems. It had an odd title, "Thoughts for Tonio." I had to read it. Like a compulsion to know something I shouldn't know, I made myself smuggle it upstairs where I also went looking for the Virginia Woolf book and then did something else I've never done before—I stole the Virginia Woolf book.

Now my life speeds down tracks with some unknown destination. What would Miss Fromm or Mrs. Wald think if they saw me now? Would they recognize this reckless Scags? Everything changes so fast here. First I am lonely and miserable and then I am this sleuth and then a thief, who does drugs. What's next? Who cares?

That's the odd thing about all of this. I don't care that I behave this way now.

It is paying off. Do you hear me, you old Scags waiting for that seedling to sprout? It is happening. My new life has finally begun to excite me. Even though my poor head is accustomed to a much quieter life, the newly sprouted Scags is finally having some fun.

I didn't want to be that sad Scags who went to the movies by herself on Saturday nights and sat in the Old Orchard Theater with a book in her hands, the same book every Saturday night, while her classmates were on dates. Over the top of the book, I spied on them as they held hands, goofed off and made out. I watched the movies, lost in them only to have to return to my life, such as it was, and walk home alone wishing things were different.

Here, all at once, the news of my new life finally reached me. I have important things to look forward to.Thank you Mama for this diary. Without it, there'd be no way for me to keep track of all these quickly changing scenarios.

I'm going to savor every part of this story as it comes tumbling out of me. I read Dr. Fish's first book of poems. Not what I had expected. Never in a million years, never, would I have imagined him sitting in a cafe watching young men walk by and wishing he could make love to one of them. Never. Where I come from, young men don't want other young men as lovers. Or if they do, they never, ever say so. And not in print.

It's not that I have anything against Dr. Fish wishing to fall in love. That's exactly what I want too. But I'm not sure I want to know the specifics of what Dr. Fish wants. I put that book back at the reserve desk as if I had found a dirty magazine under one of the chairs and couldn't quite say what it was when I turned it in. No one looked at me or said a word. That was damn lucky.

They didn't suspect either that inside my book bag was an old torn copy of the Virginia Woolf book. I had to take it. It was the only copy on the shelf and it was going to disappear. The cover on it was torn as was the spine of the book. People had drawn in the pages and all in all, it wasn't fit for the shelves.

Dr. Fish's book was old too. But it had been read and taken good care of. People must admire him, I told myself. I had looked for a time, despite how little time I had, at his photograph on the back of the book. Young, thin and wearing very similar clothes to those he wears now, Dr. Fish wasn't what I would have ever called handsome.

Of course, he was brilliant and intense. I would like to be known that way too. He looked out of the back of that book at me as he does in class—he doesn't see me at all. He doesn't want to either.

Opening the book was like walking into his house to steal his diary. Now I know things about him that I may not want to know. No, I definitely don't want to know this about him. Each moment I sat there reading his book, I knew I was in danger of missing out on sitting next to Charles at the movies.

But I couldn't stop reading. It was like when I found my parents' love letters. I knew I should put them back on their closet shelf but once I began reading, I couldn't stop. I knew what I was doing was wrong, that knowing those intimate things they shared were none of my business—it didn't matter—I couldn't stop.

For weeks, I couldn't look at them without blushing.

But who is this Scags who read through that entire book? Stole the Virginia Woolf book and then raced over to the arts building for a movie and made herself sit right next to Charles as if it were the most natural thing in the world to do. Who are you Scags?

I'm the happiest person in the world. But tomorrow, first thing, I have to find Eileen. I have a million questions to ask her about my date with Charles tomorrow night. For instance, how do I tell Charles I have no money to go out to dinner?

I found him at the movies. The movie had already begun that's how late I was. But I forced myself to sit as close to him as possible. Tony was with Charles, of course. But so few people were there. I don't get it. Free movies are like free food. Never say no to it. That is my new motto.

I sat near Charles and Tony. They were joking around with each other. The room got dark and the credits began to roll. I heard Tony say to Charles, "Hey Charles, your name sakes in this movie. Charles Foster Kane."

Charles hit him in the ribs. "Don't be a wise ass."

"Okay, I won't. But I still think it's funny your parents naming you after a character in a movie."

"It wasn't this movie, you dummy. That was 'Citizen Kane.' Now shut up."

I liked listening to them goof around with each other. It helped me relax a bit. Well, I don't think I relaxed. I watched the movie, or film, as Charles calls it, and remembered my Pops whistling that zither music. That also helped to calm me down.

I watched the film and most of the way through it, I didn't really care one way or the other what happened. It wasn't that I was bored; it just seemed to go right over my head. Until, that is, I saw, towards the end of the film the way Anna didn't care about all the awful things her man Harry Lime had done. She just wanted him to be alive. Even if she never saw him again, it didn't matter. She said something like, "Right now, Harry is alive. He is doing things."

The way she said that, it made me think that was the kind of love I was looking for. Her love for that despicable Harry Lime inspired me to speak to Charles.

Yes, I got up the nerve to speak to him and then we walked back towards the dorm and his car. Along the way, much happened that wouldn't have happened had I not seen the way Anna's eyes looked as she thought of Harry being alive. Harry who had killed all those people because of his greed. She lived inside her love, and to me, well, I've never seen anything like this before. It was almost religious on her part.

As Charles and I walked along the path that led to the dorms, I tried to explain this to him. He lit his cigarette and for several minutes we were in the film, walking along, talking about it and trying to understand it together.

In the midst of that attempt to explain my thoughts, I got cold. The nights here are now very cold and I had a jacket with me and ran into so much difficulty trying to put it on that we both laughed our heads off.

Wow. He has a wonderful laugh. I laughed so hard I began to cry and then the crying wouldn't stop. It went on and on. I knew it was for Anna. I said that.

"Anna makes me feel so sad. This love of hers is so different from anything I have seen before. I admit I don't understand it but I loved watching her feel it."

Charles then untangled my jacket and got it on me properly. We continued to the door of this dorm and stood next to it. I was afraid to break the connection that had popped up between us.

"Would you like to go to dinner tomorrow night?" Charles asked me. In such a quiet voice too for such an important question. His hands were on either side of my shoulders. It was like being pinned to the canvas, like a painting pinned to the wall. I smelled his coffee and cigarettes.

I shook my head yes and looked right into his eyes. He and I stand eye to eye. I like that. Being so tall has always been a problem for me. Charles was right there. I put my arms around him. For a moment I held tight and then broke free of him

and tried to run upstairs by getting into the doorway before he could stop me, but he stopped me.
He held the door closed and told me he would pick
me up at 7:00 tomorrow night.

He took a step back and I grabbed that door
handle and pulled it open and began to move
away. I stopped though, remembering it would
be good to say yes, and that I was happy to be
going out with him.

Happy to be going out with him? Never have
I uttered such an understatement!

Goodnight my Handsome Charles.

Now I have officially been on a date. Oh my. What a date it was. So much to tell about it and if I get it all down right, even if we never see each other again, which of course I don't want to happen, I will have this to read through so I can remember it all.

First, I had so many things to take care of on Saturday morning to get ready for this once in a lifetime experience that I barely slept on Friday night. Too excited and too worried. I had no idea how I was going to pay for this dinner. Even with the extra money Goldie sends me, well, I didn't know what it would cost. I had spent so much money already on books.

Clothes too were going to be a problem unless I got out of bed early and made sure that I had clean clothes to wear that looked presentable. For the first time in my life, I looked at my wardrobe and saw that it was a sorry story. Nothing about it told anyone who I really am. The kids here have such interesting clothing. I look like a stock character from the Midwest who has just recently learned how to apply lipstick.

I see their boots, Frye boots, and tasseled leather jackets, lots of leather all the time. Leather vests. Leather hats. Charles just has that one leather jacket but it looks so good on him. In the cold it makes a noise that sounds like feet in very cold snow.

I have solid-colored everything and my one

concession to something different for me is the collection of striped oxford cloth shirts that require lots of ironing to look nice and neat. I wore corduroy pants with an oxford cloth shirt and one of the new bulky sweaters Goldie bought me because of how cold it gets up here and boy does it ever. I thought Chicago was cold.

But even though my clothes make me feel inferior and let's face it, poor, it's the actual lack of money that weighs me down here and no more so than when I got out of bed on Saturday morning.

Boy, what an idjit I am. Girls don't pay for the dates. As soon as Alex told me that, I began to soar above everything. I was filled with helium and my sorry wardrobe and my even sorrier bank account were insignificant. Now above all that worry, I was determined to have the best date ever.

I looked around for Eileen on Saturday morning but couldn't find her. I wanted her advice about clothes and money. I went for my scheduled run when I couldn't locate her. Alex and I were the only ones who showed up. Saturdays we go for a 7-mile run. I showed up without yet having committed to being on the team. I enjoy running. I assume I can run with them whether I compete or not.

For the first 3 miles of our run, Alex didn't speak. He was annoyed that no one else had showed up. I didn't mind his silence as I was building up my courage to ask him for a loan. I hoped the opportunity to ask would just present itself.

When he asked me what I was doing for the weekend, I thanked the air around me, and started to tell him that I had been asked out on a date but didn't really have the money to pay my way.

We were running side by side at that point so I blurted my words out to the air in front of me. Alex laughed. I hadn't expected that.

"What are you some womens' libber? Don't you like it when the man pays for you? Feel like he's taken away your power or something?"

That shook me up. Out of my confusion, I said, "Hey, I'm no feminist." In all likelihood, that isn't true but as I noted, I was very confused.

"Then why are you concerned about having the money for a date?" He tried to look at me sideways but it was difficult in the terrain we were now racing through. I have no idea why the speed of our run had increased, but we were really moving along at quite a pace then.

"Well, just in case he needs me to help with the bill," I eked out of my now very confused brain. That at least seemed somewhat plausible.

"I wouldn't worry about that, my lovely Scags, and could we please reduce our speed here? This area is tricky and with all this leaf cover we could have a serious accident and be so far from the campus."

He spit into the woods and slowed down. I did too.

Back in my room, I was overcome with some-thing I never felt before—gratitude. I have felt gratitude before of course, but this was a different type of gratitude. It was like being held in the arms of good luck and not worrying about when it would drop me.

Charles showed up right on time for our date. I was ready, had been ready for at least an hour and I was starving but also afraid I would throw up when we ate.

His beat up Jeep is even more unpleasant to be in than it looks. It was dark outside when Charles came to get me. The lights don't go on inside the Jeep when you get in. Even my Mama's old Rambler has lights inside. In the darkness, I couldn't see anything. I kept banging my knees against this metal plate where the glove compartment should be. It was drafty too. Cold air rose up through the floor.

Charles drives like he owns a sports car. He is plain reckless. At the bottom of the hill at the spot where you have to turn left or right to leave the College, he frightened the pants off me. It was a foggy night. I couldn't see anything and I don't know how he could either. There's a sharp curve so the cars coming from the right aren't visible until they are coming right at you.

I held my breath as he turned right onto

the highway. Not one car came up behind us or towards us. The noise of his engine made my sigh of relief inaudible but once he got the damn thing up to speed, I started laughing about the close call we had just had. He said that wasn't true. We had had nothing to worry about. Yeah sure, I thought, he had nothing to worry about. I worried enough for both of us.

By the time we reached the Town, the fog had lifted, and I could calm down. He drove along the silent streets with his car sounding like we were an invading army. By the time he pulled into a parking lot in the middle of town, I could barely hear anything. He took my hand as soon as I got out of the car. I was too excited to object and followed him straight for the restaurant. I wanted to roam the streets in quiet with him before dinner. But he was hungry and also said he wanted a drink. I thought, oh my, good thing he's paying for all of this.

The restaurant was up a long flight of stairs. When Charles opened the door, the sound of quiet eating and drinking greeted us. No loud laughing and shouting like at the Commons, though lots of kids from the College were there.

The waiter took us to a table near the fireplace, it was really quite cozy and beautiful. He treated us both as if we were there every night. I pretended that was true and now hope that it might be.

As beautiful as the place was it made me nervous. I wanted to ask the waiter for help. I wanted to ask him why there were so many pieces of silverware on the table, so many glasses too and then why so much of it was removed as soon as we ordered our meals and drinks.

In the end, none of that was the real problem. The problem for me was I didn't know Charles and I didn't know how to talk to him. We kept trying to talk and interrupted each other. I listened to the crackling of the wood in the fire and waited for the first warmth of the wine he ordered for us to help me find something of interest to talk about.

I tried to conjure Aunt Money and have her fill me up with smart, funny things to say. Charles, it turns out, doesn't like to talk that much. It seemed like it was going to be my job to make our evening interesting.

At first I said the strangest things, things I had never said before. You know that stupid stuff we say when only cliches will do. I didn't know how to stop this avalanche of inanity. Charles was no help.

What saved me from total humiliation was Odessa's appearance at the table. She stood over us with her hands on her hips smiling at me. When she said, "Are you ready to make some sense now?" I knew the smartest thing I could do was to ask Charles about himself. After all, no matter how quiet a person is, he will gladly answer questions about himself. Charles was no exception and I finally sat back and let the man speak.

The fire was quite warm and it played along his cheekbones making him look a bit sinister one minute and then sad the next. Neither was true but he spoke softly, slowly and I can't say I paid close attention. I couldn't take my eyes off his face and the way those blue eyes worked. They are enormous, protected by these lusciously long eyelashes. It hit me that I had met a man who is beautiful, more than handsome. Sitting so close to him, I could finally see what he looked like and how his mouth moved while he spoke and what the texture of his skin was.

In the midst of answering my questions, he turned to me and asked, "Are you nervous?"

"Of course I am." I thought how obvious it must be and how nice of him to notice. "Thanks for noticing."

"It's okay. I don't bite."

He took my hand for a moment and looked at it.

"My what long fingers you have."

"All the better to scratch your eyes out with if you don't ask me out again."

We both laughed at that.

"I guess the ice is broken."

With that, we talked about things I rarely get

to talk about with anyone. Like what it was I really wanted to do with my life and why. Charles was good at asking questions too and as I relaxed into the night, as dinner came and went (I can't remember what we ate, dammit) and as the coffee and brandy sat before us, I knew this was how I was meant to live.

Charles had been a theater major and then dropped out of school to figure out if that was what he really wanted to do. Then he came back, this fall, to be a political science major with a minor in economics.

"Now that's a radical change." That was all I could say. But it was so radically different, such a different course he now charted for his future.

My plans sounded vague and fanciful, even to me. As a freshman, I am entitled to such vagueness, I told him. I had a bit more time to figure things out. The scholarship gave me the time to figure things out too.

He looked surprised when I told him I was on scholarship. I don't know why. From my clothes and all it ought to be obvious. In any case, once the surprise left his face, we continued talking about what we wanted to study.

He was full of ambition to do something more substantial with his life but felt that the war stood in the way. He is opposed to it, he told me, and wanted to work for a society that wouldn't ever choose to go to war again. He asked me if he sounded naive.

I couldn't believe he thought I would have an answer to that question. Talk about naive. I smiled and held onto his hand that he hadn't taken away since we finished dinner and gave it a squeeze.

It felt wonderful to feel so grown up. To have such a wonderful night that I hoped would never end. But of course it did. It had to.

The restaurant cleared out and we remained. The fire didn't get replenished with logs. Eventually, Charles asked for the check. I breathed a sigh of relief as he took out his wallet without even looking at me. He put a number of large bills on the table and we stood up to leave. I wanted to ask him if he didn't need to wait for the change but I kept silent and followed him through the door and down the stairs.

The night was still cold but clear. The number of stars in the sky made me realize that so much was going on as the two of us sat and talked the night away. A half moon hung right near the horizon and I wanted to go sit in it with Charles. I smelled magic and wood burning stoves in the air.

The best part was as he drove me home, he didn't speed up. He took his time. He cleared his throat and turned to look at me a lot. My eyes were on him and on the road (you can't ever be too careful).

When we got to the dorm building, he stopped the car. He said, "Don't get out yet. It's too cold to stand outside."

I let go of the door handle and sat back. He leaned over and put his face near mine, looked into my eyes and then kissed me. He did. He kissed me with his lips only and then his tongue played at my lips. Something inside me knew what to do and I responded to his kiss as if I had kissed someone every night all my life long. We kissed for a long time.

When I got out of the car, my cheeks felt reddened by his cheeks. I also had another date lined up with him for Friday night. We are seeing another film, "Brief Encounter." That's what they're showing. I don't know anything about it.

Charles said he likes that they are showing these older black and white films. I didn't care what they showed at that moment so long as it meant that I would see it with Charles.

I'm so tired now. I barely slept on Saturday night. All that food and the coffee so late at night. Then today I had my work to do for the coming week. It is a special week now. I know at the end of it, I will be seeing my Beautiful Charles.

What a week it's been so far. I wish there were time to write in here every day, but there isn't. I am both pleased with how well my work is going but upset too

On the one hand, my ability to stay focused on the work has improved after getting the week off to a bad start.

Monday, I woke up still tired from the weekend. I almost fell asleep in my classes. My runs weren't all that phenomenal until today's and that made a big impression on Alex who I think had begun to suspect that I wasn't really as good as I had said I was.

Fresh from feeling better about everything and getting closer to the time I would see Charles again, I had coffee with Eileen. That just happened by luck, but what she told me about Charles wasn't as fortunate. I had been so pleased to see her and then I was so displeased by what she told me.

Now that the two of us have something else to share with each other—our boyfriends—Eileen wanted to have a long, intense talk about Philip and Charles. Today's plan was to go over whether we were wise to hook up with these two guys. The way she talked about Philip, there was no question at all that he was Mr. Perfect. I don't believe that he is all she says he is, but she knows him and my only evidence is having seen him walk across campus holding her hand as if he owned her.

According to Eileen, both these men are "filthy rich." She has dug out information on their fathers. I have no idea who Charles' father is but Eileen informed me that he's vice-president of an oil company and is therefore, "really, really wealthy."

What other news she had to give me about Charles contradicted what he said about why he had left school and why he returned. Eileen said that Charles had been suspended for doing drugs and maybe selling drugs too. The fact that his family is so rich is why the College only suspended him for one semester.

I didn't ask her for proof. I also didn't tell her what Charles had told me. Stacked up against Eileen's Mr. Perfect, my handsome Charles isn't quite so wonderful, as Eileen sees it. Her parting words were for me to be careful and make sure he is clean before hopping into bed with him.

She walked away happy with her choice of Philip. I was left worried and alarmed. Now that I know how Eileen operates, though, I can see I have to be careful of her too.

Pops is right, some people may say they are your friend but they aren't. They are just out to see what of your soul they can steal. I'm not saying Eileen is that sort of person yet but I must keep my eye on her.

I had a dream last night and I must sort it out quickly. It really upset me.

In my dream, that didn't start out frightening but inched its way to that state, I am in this large circus tent. All of us from the College are in the tent. It is made of this opaque white material that allows lots of white light to filter in.

Charles and I are sitting on the lawn inside the tent. It is a brilliant green colored lawn that breathes as if it's breathing for all of us inside the tent. The main tent flap is tightly tied shut, from the inside.

All of a sudden, the tent flap is torn open and in step my parents. They act as if they have been invited, but I know they haven't been. Charles stands up and pulls me to my feet too.

He throws a rifle to me. He yells, "Kill them. Kill them. Now."

I don't know what to do. I look at my parents and point the rifle at them. "Why?" I ask Charles. He looks at them and back at me and says, "You know why. Why do you ask these stupid questions? Just kill them. Now."

I put the rifle up to my shoulder and look down the barrel of it. At the end of it, I see Mama and Pops back at home sitting at the kitchen table. Odessa hands them their coffee just the way they like it. I know that killing them is wrong but I want to kill them and not because Charles tells me to but because I want to kill them.

Then I shook myself awake.

I was inside the covers of my bed as if the room were freezing cold but I was so hot I thought I could set the sheets on fire. A guilty panic charged through my whole body, following the blood down every vein to the tips of my toes. The alarms in my body went off. I couldn't breathe but I had to get out of bed to end the crisis and make sure no more damage was done.

I don't remember ever feeling this amount of anger before.

I felt like a monster. I went for a run alone in the dark. I don't need bread crumbs to find my way back anymore. The faster I ran, the harder I pushed myself, I couldn't outrun the guilt. I'm really not a very nice person. I didn't know that about myself.

I'm at Charles' apartment. We had sex last night and he is still asleep. I couldn't sleep anymore. It was fantastic. I am so happy but inside me I hear these little voices going on and on about what will Mama and Pops think. That's what woke me up, this worry.

What confuses me, though, is I wasn't raised with any imposition of a specific moral code. Yet, these voices in my head make it sound as if I were.

My parents never told me not to do something because it was morally wrong. Not once did they say like the other kids' parents did—you can't do this, don't do this.

I liked Mama and Pops so much for not behaving like that. So why do I feel so guilty about sleeping with Charles? Why does this guilt feel like it could come between Charles and me?

Every cell in my body loved having sex with him. The part that isn't physical is having a harder time accepting that I'm not a virgin anymore.

It can't be because we aren't married. I've never thought about sex and marriage at all.

If I don't let the guilt take over, I know I could fall in love with Charles.

Last night, Charles and I saw "Brief Encounter." Charles thought it was a silly romantic film. Perhaps. To me, it was so poignant—that's the word—poignant. I couldn't find it last night when we came back to his place and started talking about the film. I tried to explain to him how having to live a lie can be both painful and necessary.

It's like when I read Mama's letters to Pops from when they were first dating. I know that I never should have read them. I learned things I didn't want to know. Mama's gushy pleading with Pops, for example, to be honest with her and tell her why he would be so upset for no reason at all, at least for no reason she could understand, made me watch them more closely after that. I understood how Mama could have been frightened by Pops and wonder if he was the right man for her.

Now, that I am away, she writes to me about wanting to return to that golden time when they first fell in love and I can't say anything. My most honest response to her is that I understand how something can be wonderful and awful at the same time.

I understand Mama. She thinks I don't or that I'm upset about her telling me how my being away is such a good thing for her and Pops. I'm not upset. It's just that I wish she weren't involved with making Pops out to be someone he never was. If she could be a little more realistic, I would feel comfortable asking her for some help with what's going on in my life.

For the first time, I want some motherly advice about sex. I sure as hell don't want to get pregnant. I must be like my Pops and think that for me too having a kid would destroy everything I'm working towards now. Wow. I've never thought about those letters like this before. I never saw me struggling with the same things that got my Pops so worried and then into trouble. I don't want to be like my Pops.

No wonder I can't sleep tonight.

Did I ever think about becoming pregnant before tonight? Oh Scags. What world have you walked into?

In "Brief Encounter," a married woman, Laura, meets a married doctor, Alec, at a train station. They fall in love. In this movie too, love is seen as something different from what I want love to be. I mean that just the way I wrote it here. I want this time with Charles to be wonderful and fun and tender. I don't want all that pain and worry and fear and guilt.

Yet, here I am starting out that way and we have only slept with each other once.

Charles and I had a heated argument last night about that movie. I couldn't get him to see my point. Instead of going over and over the same thing with me, he made me get up off the couch and follow him into his bedroom. By moving into that room, we finally could be loving with each other. It was really beautiful. I know what a banal thing that is to say, but having never slept with anyone before, it was like getting inside my body in such a new way that made running seem pointless. In bed with Charles, I experienced all the parts of my body without having to worry at all about getting injured or pushing myself too hard. It wasn't about my body either but about the two of us having bodies. I never realized that was what sex was like. I have to think about this more so I can describe it better.

I think I'm also afraid that just as easily as I am beginning to fall in love with Charles, I could just as easily fall out of love with him. It's not him I don't trust, but me.

These are among the things I'd like to talk to Mama about. The myriad things that are happening that I don't understand and make me question what I'm walking into. I require balance in my life and this is certainly about to take that away.

I want to tell Mama about how I rolled over in bed the other night and almost fell out of it, because I was grabbing to hold onto Charles but he wasn't there. I caught myself and didn't fall flat onto the floor. I want her to tell me why these things are happening to me.

Mama could tell me why falling in love is so troubling while being fun too. Why must everything turn into a trial? Am I being tested to see if I am good enough to love someone? Did she feel that way when she met Pops?

Okay. I hear Charles getting out of bed. I'm going to stop writing now.

More later. I promise.

I'm at the library now. I spent most of this week-end with Charles.

What's going on? It doesn't matter. Just listen, if you don't get your work completed, you will fail and lose this glorious scholarship and have to leave College and Charles. So buckle down and do your work.

I'm promising myself that right now. First I must write this down: Charles and I are going to a doctor so I can get a prescription for birth control pills. Being Charles' lover got complicated quickly.

Okay. To work or else.

I'm pleased to report that I'm back on track for now. I stayed until very late at the library last night and caught up with everything I wanted to work on. Since two of my classes are purely academic in structure, I know how to study for them. It may be a bit time consuming but at least I am clear about what needs to be done and how to get it all done on time. I enjoy both the Psychology and Philosophy courses.

They're not as challenging as I thought they would be. I assumed that my classmates' private school educations would trump my public school one. But my formulas keep me always ahead and aware of what needs to be covered. I give myself plenty of time to digest it too.

It's rewarding to be at the top of the classes.

In contrast to the rows of seats we sat in at Niles North, here at the College, we sit around large wooden tables. Each classroom is set up that way. There are only 12 students per class. I like not talking to the backs of other students' heads when I answer a question. We can look at each other and discuss the work rather than only respond to the professor's questions.

However, as always, there are those anomalies. Need I say who? As always—Dr. Fish and Prof. Calderon.

Dr. Fish's poetry class is the most disturbing one. His comments in class always make me feel inferior. He never deviates at all from his theory that women aren't qualified to read poetry let alone write it.

When I walk out of his classroom, I am convinced that this will be my one and only term here. It takes hours of work for me to trust that I can pass his course and be true to myself in the work. If nothing else, I have mastered new skills as a student to make my work for the odious old fuck face presentable.

While working on my papers for his class, I want to suggest to him that I could be a writer. I want to suggest to him that I could make a living as a writer. Plainly, his course, I would tell him, has taught me that already.

I feel foolish describing what goes on in his class in my diary. I waste my own time here just as he does. Listening to Dr. Fish repeating often his belief that women can't write poetry and shouldn't be allowed in discussions of it, I know my blood rushes straight to my face, neck and hands. Being a red head creates some dangerous problems. People are aware, sometimes before I am, how angry I am. I know he has observed my red face response in reaction to his stupid ideas.

In his class, by the way, we don't sit around the table. There is no table. He has a podium at the front of the room. He appears at some point right when he thinks he should show up, places his books onto the podium and stares at them. He looks like a walrus. He dresses in the same standard issue clothing each day—brown corduroy jacket, knit tie, checkered shirt, grey trousers and saddle shoes. He makes harumphing walrus sounds as if he prepares to start the class. He looks around, surprised that no one has left. Then he plows ahead with his prepared remarks and ignores any raised hands until he has completed what he has decided to say to us that day.

He jettisoned some of the assignments that were on his original syllabus to make room for Coleridge's Conversation Poems. I don't mind as I like them and I'm going to write my term paper on one of them. There's a rumor that the reason he changed the syllabus is he's writing an article about these poems and needs the class to help with his article.

Even though he has that academic side to him, there are those days, like today, when we come to class prepared to work but he stops what he is lecturing about to become weird.

Today, Dr. Fish stopped talking about Coleridge in mid-sentence and counted all the women in the room.

He closed his book, stepped away from the podium, and said, "No woman sitting in this room should take it into her head to become a poet. It is not possible, not physically or mentally possible for a woman to write poetry of any kind."

I don't know why he says those things but the room goes still when he does.

His lectures are brilliant but the room goes so still when he behaves like that. No one feels comfortable sitting there.

When he stopped talking about the inability of women to write poetry, he then told us about a conversation he had with Coleridge last night. It's truly a bizarre experience to listen to him recite these stories. We've heard them before because whenever he veers off from his lecture, he tells us these exact stories, every time.

Collectively, we know he is both brilliant and a nut case. On top of that he is a misogynist.

I told Neal, who sits next to me in the class that I call Dr. Fish "Old Fuck Face." He told me that was a perfect description and then proceeded to tell others in the class of my renaming of Dr. Fish. Everyone whispers "Old Fuck Face" as we leave his classroom. Someone will say, "Did you hear Old Fuck Face say that he talks to Coleridge at night?" We hold our breaths, afraid that Old Fuck Face heard us. Once we are out of earshot, we laugh to expel the horrible tension he stirs up in us.

I know if I could make myself sit down to read 'A Room of One's Own' I will feel better. Eileen assures me I will. I don't know why I'm afraid to pick up that book and see what Woolf has to say about men like Dr. Fish. Tonight, I must crack it open or I stole that damn book for no reason.

While I am explaining the differences in my classes, I should mention that my pottery class is also completely different from the academic classes. First of all, it isn't a class I can study for. Not in the classical sense of study.

Prof. Calderon talks so much about beauty and how beauty is found, who creates it, and why. You listen to her say that word, beauty, and it's now a new language that I am learning. Very different from what I had thought this class was going to be. (I should go and thank Prof. Keating for making me take this class. He would probably be pleased to know how much I like it.)

Not unlike how my Aunt Money charges up a room with her perfume, Prof. Calderon makes a room fire up with her excitement for throwing pots.

She talks about the art and science of clay and of beauty. She embodies that too. The one thing I see in my mind whenever I think of her class is how she took her fingers along the side of a small pot and showed that curve, the roundness of it, the way a woman might touch her own swollen belly when pregnant.

I blurted out that thought. She didn't know who said it. She whirled around looking at the room and asked who had uttered those words?

I raised my hand. She stared at me for a few seconds before saying, "Excellent comment Scags. Making that direct connection to the power of clay to show fecundity is essential to understanding its purpose."

She smiled right at me. "I expect you to continue letting us hear your insights."

I must have blushed and turned completely red because she said, "Don't worry, Scags. We'll all help you find that power here. That's why we structure the class this way."

Then she returned to holding the pots and showing us things about them that I couldn't pay any attention to. I had become too self-conscious. Looking around the room to help me divert my thoughts, I noticed that the entire room was filled with women. Not one man had signed up for the class. Maybe beauty is a frightening topic for a man to discuss.

I was granted one easy class. That's the Phys. Ed class. I don't worry about it or even think about it. I get up and run with the team every morning. I feel so lucky to have this gorgeous woodland to float through. The colors are more robust than any I have ever seen in the Fall. Though I was told that once the leaves are gone, this is also a bleak landscape. We shall see.

The sounds of the leaves underfoot make me feel like I am getting things done. It's as if I were going places and seeing things I never saw before even when I run pretty much the same course every day.

Alex paired me with Douglas. We run side by side every day. He's not new here but he can't believe how beautiful the woods are too. We gobble up the sights of it and compare what we have seen from day to day. Soon the woods will look differ-ent and there will be much less light. I don't care about that at all.

I like running in the mountains rather than on flat land. Yes, it is more rigorous than running in Skokie. I even had the shit scared out of me when one morning, a huge owl hovered over me. I saw its enormous talons hanging near my head and wondered what it would be like to be scooped up by and dragged off to its nest. The wingspan was about 10 feet. I mean it. It felt mythic or maybe even like a dinosaur had returned to find its way into the modern world. Douglas told me that they can scoop up baby calves. Or dogs. Once, they saw a bear out on the trails. You definitely have to be careful.

I stole Virginia Woolf's "A Room of One's Own" back into the library so I could read it tonight during a break in my studies. That was a huge mistake. Reading that book took over my whole night. It is now one of the books that changed my life. I became so involved in the book, they had to kick me out of the library.

I put my stolen book back into my book bag and walked into the cold, night air. I fell in love with her sentences. They're like drugs that alter how I perceive sentences, how I can describe my thinking and the differences between men and women.

I didn't want to return to my room as I walked out of the library. Coming back up here would have seemed too normal for the thoughts that were tumbling around inside my head. I had nowhere to go. The Commons lights were on but it looked too bright and festive in there. I needed quiet and the dark.

I walked around outside in the dark. I threw my head back to look at the stars. They were so numerous it was as if I had thrown fistfuls of jacks into the night air with all my might. Each one glowed back at me as if their tips had been set on fire. I reached out to them, asking them to follow me. Waving my arms at them, they ricocheted all over the black bowl above my head. The entire expanse was mine. I owned it. In large circles as they bounced against the sides of that huge bowl, they responded to every move I directed them to make.

I wanted to see the whole sky all at once. But that made me dizzy. Both the wonder of that huge sky with its dazzling lights as well as my attempts to see it all made me feel that if I didn't come upstairs and write down what is happening to me, I would never be able to capture so much magic again. It was like a challenge that my life makes now—experience everything but don't forget to write it down too.

I'm glad Sylvie was out for the night.

First, I want to copy into this book some of what I read tonight. By writing it in my own handwriting, it will be more mine. The feel of my pen along the paper does something to me too. It opens a writing door and makes me peek inside. These sentences aren't mine but I am communing with them when I do this simple exercise. I watch them exist in a different place than the book page.

> *Thought—to*
> *call it by a prouder name than it*
> *deserved—had let its line down into*
> *the stream. It swayed, minute after minute,*
> *hither and thither among the*
> *reflections and the weeds, letting the*
> *water lift it and sink it*
> *until—you know the little tug—the*

sudden conglomeration of an idea at
the end of one's line: and then the cautious
hauling of it in, and the
careful laying of it out? Alas, laid on the
grass how small, how
insignificant this thought of mine looked;
the sort of fish that a good
fisherman puts back into the water so that
it may grow fatter and be one
day worth cooking and eating. I will not
trouble you with that thought
now, though if you look carefully you may
find it for yourselves in the
course of what I am going to say.

I ran my eyes over the words before copying them into this diary. I hope to fall asleep tonight and see them dancing across a black bowl, like my stars, as I drift off.

Each word, as I wrote it down, reverberated in me. So many ideas came bounding into my mind like numerous telegraphs leading to places inside me I hadn't known existed. I can't stop them from poking at me and urging me to pay attention to them.

One thing is clear: Before I read her essay, my life had the form of a series of distinct points on a line—events, things happened, one after the other, in the manner of this happened and then that happened. I did this. I did that. I haven't done this but will do it. Everything neatly arranged. Life appeared to be a line that led somewhere, taking me somewhere based on what I did. Or didn't do.

But reading her description of thought opened up something else. Now like huge church bells tolling inside my head and knocking all that order out of order, making me far more aware of how necessary real change must be.

This is difficult to believe, but even more powerfully than Mr. Lowell's poems, her prose description of thought as a fish pulled out of the water before it had grown to its full size hit me hard. More than Mr. Lowell's poem making me realize how essential the personal is to poetry, her essay is making me feel that here, at College, I am that fish caught too soon. What I am and what I know are not yet mature.

Now I must go slowly through her entire book. If ever I felt a book spoke its entire message to me and to me alone, this is it.

Tuesday night has almost ended I see. What a glorious way to spend the time. Do I care that my work will suffer tomorrow? Do I care that I may not run well? That I may fail the trials for the first race?

In my psych class we have begun to read Freud and his interpretation of Oedipus Rex. There we discuss an Oedipal complex as it relates to men.

In my philosophy class we have begun reading Plato, the Symposium, his dialog about love. But the love is among men, no women are mentioned.

What a life of the mind I am being ushered into. Woolf is helping me to see that these are men's ideas and not necessarily applicable to how women think, feel or perceive the lives they live.

With her warning about taking all of this male erudition too seriously, I am like a young child. I want to become the person who is influencing me the most.

While I don't know where this will lead me, I am eager to let it rumble around and see how it might change me. Maybe I will dream about Woolf. Maybe she'll send me a message in my dreams about how I should use her ideas in my life.

That would certainly cut down my worry that I'll never live up to her standards.

Harvest Moon time here in Vermont. I miss Mama and Pops and our ritual celebration of that over-sized moon. I now have to celebrate the Harvest Moon alone.

There's no one to make the ritual come alive with me. It's really just a Morgenstern celebration. Who else would do what we do- parade in circles, watching the moon rise above us, inviting us to fly to it? Of course we always turned down her invitation. But she never revokes it.

I saw the Harvest Moon rise this evening as I walked from Commons after dinner on my way to the library. The people here are too sophisticated to dance with me singing made up songs to the moon. I'd be afraid to invite them to join me.

We Morgensterns are aware of what people think of us. We're the crazies on the block. In all of Skokie, we were seen as the craziest in the entire suburb.

Pops made the rising of the Harvest Moon a holiday for us because the moon frightened me. There was no way to explain that to our neighbors. Each fall as we made a feast night of it, the looks we got from our neighbors, even the Arthurs, made it clear that our moon worship antagonized them.

Pops soaped the word "awe" that night on our living room window. In large letters he put it out there for people to contemplate, as he put it. He also drew the big moon, in all her redness, on our front window. He didn't see the difference between Halloween decorations and our hailing of the rising of the Harvest Moon.

I miss our family's inventiveness. I must remember to carry on that tradition here. In my own way of course and with my own events to celebrate.

Suddenly, I want to possess Charles. The more I see him, the more I want to possess him. Who would have thought that was even possible? I mean, how the hell long have I known him? I become annoyed when what I want to do and what he wants don't coincide. Can you believe that? I mean, who is this girl, Scags, and where did she learn to behave this way?

I watch myself now with Charles. He and the rest of the College were all lit up today because of the celebrations in honor of the release of the new Beatles album—Abbey Road.

Do I care? No. Must I? Perhaps. That has now become my new conundrum. How to make room inside me for what Charles wants as well as taking care of my needs too. Now more of my needs seem to be dependent on him.

Reading Virginia Woolf and becoming involved with my first boyfriend at the same time have definitely raised serious questions in my own mind about who I am and what it is I am supposed to be doing here.

Charles wanted his friends at his apartment. As usual, they got stoned and listened to the new album all night long.

What was I supposed to say when this wasn't how I wanted to spend my Wednesday night?

A part of me woke up to how angry this makes me feel because I feel shut out. This isn't how

I want to spend my time with him or with his friends. The truth is, I didn't want to spend time with any of these other people at all.

I don't have lots of free time. When I am not studying or running, I want to be with Charles and be right next to him. I do mean right next to him, cuddling on the couch, watching television or in bed.

I've told Charles that is what people do who have just started loving each other. They hang onto each other for dear life. He finds that idea very funny.

"You make it sound like falling in love is like drowning in a swimming pool."

"Do I? Well, that isn't exactly the image I would use."

"You wouldn't?" he asks and throws himself on the couch and yells for me to come save him.

I don't. I throw pillows at him and accuse him of not taking me seriously.

These semi-quarrels are fun. But they haven't helped me climb out of the rut I am in with him. He never excludes me from anything and yet, if he didn't spend as much time with his friends, he could reasonably spend more time with me.

"You can have all of me," he laughs and he runs into the bedroom to bring me a present. He always has some trinket that is truly very lovely and thoughtful to hand me as we fight over these silly things. I own a beautiful hand-stitched wallet. A silver bracelet and a matching pin.

Now it bothers me that I've not asked Charles about the drugs and if that was why he was away from the College. No one has ever said a word about it except Eileen. Not even in the conversations Charles and Tony have when I'm around is there any mention of that. I wonder though where all the money comes from for us to do what we do or for the presents and the apartment.

I didn't know what to say when Eileen told me about Charles' drug use.

I didn't take drugs at home and I don't intend to take many here. I tried pot with Eileen and smoke it occasionally with Charles. He and Tony take drugs, I'm sure of that. However, if Charles had been suspended for drugs, would he be so foolish as to continue once he returned to school?

I know that the two of them worry a great deal about the draft, about having to go to war. I imagine if he's drafted, I'll need to take something to deal with my anxiety about him being killed. I don't even know how to write these thoughts down. It intersects too with how Virginia Woolf wrote about the changes that occurred after the First World War in the way men and women talked to each other. Somehow everything she wrote about matches what I am dealing with now.

My imagination is fragile tonight. It wants to

run away with stories of death and destruction. If I let it do that, by the time all his guests leave and he comes to bed, he won't recognize me. I know I'm capable of transforming myself into an awful shrew who wants to chew up all the good feelings and spit them in his face. Inside of me, there is that constant tug of war between needing him to assure me that he loves me and me not wanting to discover that I may not love him.

At home, these rages came upon me when I worried about leaving Skokie. I needed reassurance that I would indeed leave. That this wasn't a cruel hoax being played on me. One night it got so bad that Mama made me take one of Pops' sedatives so I would go to bed and leave her alone.

That experience taught me a lesson. The first thing I discovered was how hard it is to get out of bed when I have taken a sleeping pill. I thought I had exiled that person for good after seeing what it took to quiet her down.

Now she turns up frequently as I fall in love with Charles. If I'm going to succumb to the drug culture because of these feelings for Charles, then I must find some other way to get through this or I will be a mess.

Midwesterners, I tell myself, don't need drugs. We are made of a sturdier form of molecular composition that allows us more resilience than these East Coast snobs.

Like Bartleby, "I prefer not to."

Now I understand why I got angry about this party. I associate The Beatles with drugs. I do. Sitting up all night listening to their new album means that they'll all be taking drugs. I know that's what makes me upset and at the same time, I really don't want to know about it. I have gotten to this place due to my hard work and I can't let this love affair or the drugs or anything side track me from the goal—four years of a free education.

For now, I am going to lie here waiting for Charles to come to bed. If I'm asleep, he'll wake me up and we'll make love. I know that. I'll fall back to sleep in his arms and worry less about things until I wake up. I sleep so well in his arms.

Charles and I are going to the doctor tomorrow to get birth control pills. I'm nervous about that too. For one thing, I can't afford them so Charles is paying for everything, including the doctor visit. This is Scags Morgenstern's new life. I have really left Skokie far behind.

Yesterday seems like a long time ago. Time stretches back to a point right after we left the doctor's office and drove to the drug store to buy the Pill. Previously, the Scags who was in love with Charles, was a student at the College and had been a daughter in the Morgenstern family, her life has now taken on new dimensions. It's like that image in my head of Odessa kneading dough to bake bread. How she has to stretch the dough in all these directions and how it stays dough but is altered. It is going to be made into something greater than the uncooked dough that has to be kneaded to be baked.

In a sentence, If ever there was a day that made me see the difference between my old world in Skokie and my new one here—yesterday was that day.

When Mama handed me this diary as I got on the train in Chicago, she never could have foreseen the enormous changes that would occur and how quickly.

If she could have hidden secret messages inside these pages about what my new life would be like, could she have written what it's like to go to a gynecologist for the first time and to be put on the Pill? Would she have been shown the materials this doctor had in her office documenting the horrors of illegal abortions and the resulting deaths?

I would have been so grateful had Mama

written in here: "Scags when you find your new boyfriend, make sure he takes you to the doctor so you can be on the Pill. Those nasty condoms are messy and can break. You're a lucky girl, my darling daughter, you can take the Pill and never have to worry again that your fun with Charles will be interrupted by an unwanted pregnancy."

I don't want sex to be about having fun or even mostly about having fun. I worry what would happen were I to become pregnant. Reading Virginia Woolf's description of Mrs. Seaton's life and her 13 children made me realize that one can't contribute to the world while worrying about all one's children. If there is one thing Charles is teaching me it's that I want to use my time on Earth to contribute rather than to only succeed.

The doctor I saw is one of the only doctors here in Town. She's an older woman who has been in this community all her professional life. Evidence of her involvement in the community was posted on all the walls along with her diplomas and degrees and licenses.

In the way she examined me and in her questions, I saw how limited her time must be with all her "well" patients. She was abrupt, yes, but also gentle. Having a waiting room filled with patients, you can't spend endless time gossiping with each patient on your examining table.

The doctor told me I was in perfect health. I knew that. She prescribed a birth control pill for me and told me to come back if I have any problems with it or in 6 months to refill the prescription. She also warned me to remember to take it faithfully or that it wouldn't work. I wanted to tell her that was going to be the only problem I would have—remembering to take it. I zipped it, though, as Goldie would have advised and left her office with a clean bill of health and a prescription for the Pill in my purse.

Charles took my hand as we walked down the street to the drug store. I felt awkward being with Charles after the examination. All of a sudden, it became real to me that being in love with him had consequences. I never thought that falling in love would also feel like that, that I had responsibilities. In the drug store, it felt like everyone watched us go to the pharmacist to have the prescription filled. Having all eyes turned to us, made me feel like petal after petal was opening on a flower and I wasn't going to ever arrive at the center of it and be able to experience its core.

I am relieved to have gotten that examination out of the way but I still worry about having to tell Mama and Pops at some point about Charles and me.

It feels like I'm whispering as I write this but Charles was very tender with me last night when we made love. It was as if he knew that a milestone had been passed. We came home and he had set up the bedroom. Candles waited to be lit. The bed had been heaped with many pillows. A bottle of wine sat on the bedside table with two glasses waiting to be filled.

After we made love, he fell asleep. I pulled back the covers to look at his naked body. It looked so vulnerable lying next to me not knowing how I was examining it. In the glow of the candles he looked sculpted and bronzed. I ran my fingers down his long back and across his small buttocks and down his legs to the ankles. He never moved. I wrote on his back with my fingers messages of how I felt from moment to moment. I wanted to believe these messages passed through his skin and into his psyche, received with all the love and trepidation with which they were sent.

I know that melancholy after lovemaking. I like it but it keeps me awake. When I don't feel it, I fall asleep in Charles' arms.

Tonight, I am awake and thinking and worrying about what I am going to do with my life. I won't be pregnant now unless I choose to be. I almost didn't have time to worry about that. Everything happens much faster in my life now.

Alex is the best running partner. In a way he is slow. I don't mean that he can't move quickly but that when he runs, he isn't working out so many things in his head at once that he feels speeded up like so many of us do.

He and I never compete. Though sometimes I want to challenge him. But as I speed up my pace, he tells me to slow it down. No sense getting hurt. For me, this team work is going to be for fun. I haven't had the heart to tell him yet that I can't join the team but I decided today to tell him. I didn't like having that indecision weigh so heavily on me.

I signed up to run with him today and it turned out to be just the two of us. No one else wanted to run in the rain. I never mind running in the rain or the snow. It is always a great challenge and it makes me aware of things I never would know if I didn't run.

Alex has also become this wonderful resource. Running with him can be like a way to map what is happening in my mind by popping up a word between us as we follow the paths and see where it leads.

Another cool thing about Alex is his sensitivity to women runners. He has coached so many women that he understands better than we do at times how our menstrual cycle affects our performance. He's never embarrassed to talk about anything that pertains to running. He knows how that strange weight in the center of a woman's body can alter how we are. He knows that has to be dealt with. No matter how lean we are, we have that womb and our hormones. Our bodies work different from mens. He is very helpful. I never knew how breathing could help me overcome menstrual cramps during a run. With the amount of pain I occasionally have, I have always stopped running. Now I know what stretches will relieve the pressure in my lower back.

I have come to depend on him too to help me with some of my problems because he seems so capable of understanding what I am going through.

First he helped me with the food problems. There is so much food served to us every day that I feared blowing up like a blimp. He taught me how to dish out servings to myself that I needed rather than just eating because it was fun or tasted good.

Then there was the menstrual problem and now it is needing to be able to run with the team without any expectation that I will compete.

I didn't want to let him know that something bothered me. Though he's quite intuitive.

"Isn't sex a funny word?" he asked me before I could pop up the courage to explain to him why I couldn't be part of the team. We were running uphill, past the faculty housing and then into the woods.

"The way it sounds or what it means?" I asked.

"I don't know. What do you think?"

I had to think through why he began our run with that question. I hadn't thought of anything other than what I needed to talk to him about so his question threw me off guard. I remained silent.

We ran side by side on the trail. This section is that wide. It made talking much easier.

He said, "I used to think that having sex was what it meant to be in love with someone. If you fucked, that was it. That was what anyone wanted and that was enough."

Wow, I thought to myself, has he been reading my mind?

"I really didn't know what it meant to be in love until I really fell in love. That changed everything."

We kept running. Neither of us spoke. I wanted to tell him that I was in love.

"Are you in love?" he asked me.

I told him I was. I told him about Charles.

He shook his head and turned to look at me. "You sure know how to pick 'em."

I asked him what he meant by that. I realized that he was about to tell me things about Charles I didn't want to hear. I wanted to stop the conversation at that point but in the rhythm of our run it was difficult to change the topic as difficult as it was to change our course.

"I don't want to make you unhappy. You are a great kid and you are so smart. How the hell did you fall for that guy?"

I didn't expect to hear him say these things. Tears weren't going to dissuade him from continuing this talk.

"I love him Alex." That was all I could say.

"Yep. love," he said. "It's a killer. Not at all what you think it is going to be. Sure as hell not like in the movies, is it?"

"Even though we want it to be."

"You got that right."

I finally got Alex to tell me why he didn't like Charles. The damn drugs issue came up again. I swore to him that Charles wasn't like that anymore. Yes, he smoked some pot and dropped some acid from time to time but he was basically clean.

Alex looked at me as if he couldn't possibly explain to me what he was thinking. He made me feel like I didn't know what I was talking about. I did know. I practically live with Charles. I would know if he was really that involved in drugs again.

When we ended the run, I walked away without saying another word to him. He waited for me to say something but I refused. On the one hand, I didn't want to defend Charles and on the other hand I was worried that I might be wrong.

Charles, Tony and I spend more time together now. We're a threesome. How quickly Charles and I moved from being together just the two of us to this threesome. The three of us eat together. We go to the movies together. We go to parties together.

I'm not angry at Charles about that change. In some ways, it is good, because now there is another voice to listen to when it comes to the political discussions we have. Charles is adamant about what he believes the truth to be. Tony has a more middle of the road attitude and is willing to listen to both sides of an argument.

The three of us were talking the other night about how women deal with things. Charles mentioned how I not only read Virginia Woolf but had also stolen one of her books. He was trying to make fun of me and my feminist ideas. But the joke backfired because the only way he could have known I had stolen that book was to have read my diary.

As soon as he spoke those words, my face went completely red. So did his. He knew he had been caught.

The competition inside me for words to shout at him caused me to say nothing. I didn't have anything to say. He reached out to me, we were sitting on the couch in his apartment. I moved away and went into the bedroom. I needed to resolve the war inside me before looking at him again. I knew I could either be insanely upset and leave or I could stay and try to salvage from this what there was. In either case, I knew I had to put the diary in places he didn't know about.

At that moment, I tried to remember how much I had loved him in the split second before he announced he had betrayed me.

All the fights we hadn't had about my suspicions about the drugs were sure to come up now. All my fears of being in love were known to him.

Even those areas of my life he isn't in were going to be up for discussion. I could see the whole cascade of problems about to begin and I wondered if I would have the energy to keep up with it. It depended, I realized, on whether I wanted to stay involved with him.

In so many ways that has been my problem all along. I don't know what it's like to really be in love with someone. I don't know if I need Charles the way Eileen seems to need Philip. I don't even know what love is supposed to be all about.

I don't know. I'm watching myself in a movie. I've come to a fork in the road and I have to choose which way to go.

The first choice is to go off alone and say fuck it all. I don't need this shit. I can be alone now and be lonely.

The other choice I can make is to continue seeing Charles if only because I won't be alone.

My character may need to use Charles to keep me company. But a more sinister side opens up on that road. I know that by choosing to walk down that road with Charles, he offers me a way into his bounteous world and that world has more than I can ever offer myself.

I see no reason not to be an opportunist. I hear these kids talk about this way of life all the time and know I have no other way into it. Why shouldn't I want to have and do things like the students all around me have? They can go into New York whenever they want to. I am stuck up here like in a prison due to my poverty. I'm sick of the jealousy I fight against. I'm even tired of not saying I am jealous.

I stayed in the bedroom for a long time. I heard Tony and Charles whispering to each other and then Tony left. Charles began cleaning up the living room and then started washing the dishes we had left in the sink. I sat upright on the bed trying to figure out what had happened and why.

It got late. I picked up my book bag and my overnight bag and packed them. Time to head out to the library, and that was in the plans all along. So it wasn't as if I was just walking out on him.

I opened the bedroom door and saw him in the kitchen, wiping down the counters as he does when he finishes the dishes. He looked at me. I tried to smile but couldn't. My mouth refused to curl upwards. In as few motions as I could take, I put on my jacket, zipped it up and flung my bags over my shoulder and walked out the door.

I left him standing in the kitchen. He didn't say a word.

I went to the library and worked most of the night. It wasn't as easy as I hoped it would be to concentrate on my assignments but eventually all thoughts of Charles receded so I could finish the work left for the weekend. Knowing I was completely up to date was going to help me get through the week.

I was pleased with how much I accomplished. Not anything more than that feeling went through me. I had blocked all thoughts of Charles from my mind. I had to or I would have been sitting in the library foolishly wasting my time.

When I returned, I found Charles waiting outside the dormitory for me.

It was cold outside and I was so tired. He wanted me to come back with him to the apartment but I told him no. I needed to stay on campus and get up early to work and to run.

He put his arms around me. Talking for him sometimes is hard. It is as if someone had told him never to say a word. But then it all spilled out of him. I felt like he removed the cork just for me.

It was like he had been running and felt the release from himself that running can give.

He apologized and apologized. He told me how horrible he felt and how empty the place felt without me in it. He did go on and on and for some reason I do believe him and I do love him and I think he just did what he said he did—gave into the temptation because it was sitting right there on the table and he always saw me writing in it and . . .

He had a present for me. He knew how much I loved his bomber jacket and would wear it when he didn't. He and I have almost the same birthday. His is April 24 and mine is April 25. But he said my birthday was too far off.

He got out this huge box and inside it was a bomber jacket for me. I couldn't believe it. I had to try it on right then. It fit perfectly and I started to cry.

It was my birthday, Christmas and Hanukkah all rolled into one. He didn't mean it, I could see it. He didn't mean to be mean.

My Handsome Harry. I love you so.

I have discovered a love for my pottery class. We're all women in the class, and Prof. Calderon is an extremely cool person. So different from any teacher I've had.

I like the way she gets to the heart of things. Being solely in the company of women is great.

She is also very dramatic and attractive. Not like Eileen is dramatic because she is a performer. She is dramatic and powerful because of how she is so in tune with her subject matter and how it affects her life.

She's not like Virginia Woolf either. Prof. Calderon comes across as being free, without cares about what anyone thinks. I believe it has to do with her own love of her sexuality. The more I study Virginia Woolf the more this weight attaches to her. Not the weight of boredom, but of oppression. She felt it so deeply.

Also, I don't know, was Virginia Woolf ever lazy, did she ever feel like being nothing other than a slug for days on end? I need to read more of her work, but I sense that it was very hard to live up to the standards she set for herself.

But it isn't just this classroom full of women that has me caught up. I guess it is that we discuss things I never would have been comfortable discussing before. Feminism wasn't a greatly appreciated idea where I come from. It conjured women who burned their bras, didn't shave their legs and might of all things be a lesbian. I realize that was a caricature but it was a strong enough one to make none of us talk about it, ever. It wasn't worth being branded with that identity.

Here at the College, there are some really strident women who people in Skokie would prefer not to know about. They aren't just loud and angry but talk about men and confront them with things that would drive the men I know at home crazy. And out of the room and down the road and as far away from them as possible.

Annette, who is in Prof. Calderon's class is one of the more strident ones. She is always posting signs for rallies, coffee house meetings. Lectures. I don't know how she has time to study but she does and does well.

She looks like a large magnet that attracts everything in her path. Whatever she has eaten, whatever she has read, wherever she has put herself, all of it clings to her.

However, when she talks, she is clear as a bell in what she believes. In Prof. Calderon's class, it is her voice I listen for when the topic of feminism comes up, which it does often. Maybe because she is in the room.

I used to blush whenever she spoke. Some of her friends, like Julie, also chime in and they have what I call a united vision. They believe exactly the same things and talk about it in exactly the same language.

I've never run across this type of friendship between women before. In some ways when they speak it is like watching a play.

Prof. Calderon used the words truth and beauty the other day. I think it was in reference to the Keats poem, "Ode on a Grecian Urn."

She was describing a technique, funny how I can't recall the specifics of this, but as soon as the words left her mouth, first Annette and then Julie spoke about how traditional forms of female beauty have been sold to women in order to enslave them.

I probably am grossly misrepresenting their ideas here. I can't yet describe how they enter into these talks, almost like bullies, except that they're not. They say some of the most thought provoking things I have heard, and then make me uncomfortable with how angry they are at men.

Maybe reading Virginia Woolf in conjunction with these experiences has forced me to reconsider things in ways I hadn't thought about and for reasons that I'm not sure I understand.

For example, and this bothers me more than Annette being angry at men. I see her point often. It's that when I look to the past, I see how not that long ago, women's lives were god awful compared to how we live today.

Woolf describes Jane Austen writing in her

room and having to hide her writing so that no one sees it. Her writing was a secret and she would never travel beyond the world she saw outside her windows.

Here we are in our classes, planning to do things in the world, while Jane Austen wrote novels she never knew would alter so many women's lives.

I read this back to myself and I know I'm not clear at all.

I know I lived in that kind of fog in high school. I also knew my life would change. Jane Austen didn't think hers would change and it didn't. Maybe I don't really deserve all that I have been given.

Can anyone help me with this problem? In the Keats poem, there's the image of those frozen people on that vase, dancing but caught dancing in that one pose never to move again. I believe they felt the joy of it, as if there were no tomorrow. So was Keats correct when he wrote: "Beauty is Truth, Truth Beauty and that is all ye need to know?"

Because I don't know.

In high school, the focus was on what things meant. We never learned how anything was made. The message, the message, that was what we had to be able to understand. Our classes became battlegrounds over meaning without us ever knowing for certain if our arguments meant anything. We enjoyed the battle.

Here, arguments turn into something far more serious. Those engaged in them seem to care personally about whether you agree with them.

Even when the things they argue about are as silly as the kind of person they believe a certain professor to be. They ridicule Prof. Loomis, our Philosophy teacher for example. They make fun of his two suits and three sweaters and one tie. They make jokes about how much underwear he owns. About how he combs his hair to hide the baldness, his one form of vanity. To them, he represents a certain type of authority figure who disdains luxury for the pure pursuit of knowledge. They find this old fashioned and paternalistic.

His clothing and austerity don't bother me. I appreciate him for being a repository of thought and study. That inside that clothing, his being has stored up many, many years of study and organized it so he could teach it to us.

His class, however, never makes me think the way Prof. Calderon's class does. In his class, I am the student. In hers I feel more like, what? Not really a student in the traditional sense.

In her extravagant clothing, the many-colored scarves, the light colored and then dark colored layers of fabric that cover her, in the perfumes she wears and the multiple pieces of jewelry she created for herself, I see, I guess, a messenger of some kind.

A form who comes to us to bring news of something else than what we hear from the rest of the world. I know that sounds very radical coming from me. Maybe it's not true and utterly worthless as an idea. It's only my way of saying that her class has taken over a part of my thought process that is escorting me to places I don't know anything about, yet.

Charles, Tony and I were hanging out at the apartment tonight. I don't usually pay attention to the things they talk about—sports, bands, drugs, sports, politics, sports. Charles and I have a completely different repertoire of topics.

Tony, to me, is a mental midget. I never talk to him about anything except to ask him to pass the salt or help me carry the groceries up the stairs.

He and Charles worked on their stage set assignment tonight on the big table in the living room. I was doing the dishes and cleaning up the kitchen after our dinner.

Tony asked Charles why he didn't act anymore. I forgot that Charles had dropped out of the theater program and became a political science major when he returned to the College. He kept his hand in the game, as he put it, by taking scene building classes. He enjoys helping with the production of the plays but not the acting.

Charles took a long time to answer Tony. I thought he might never have an answer to the question. I sure was eager to hear the answer though. It surprised me.

"I had a hard enough time knowing who I was or am most days so that going on the stage to be someone else and then to have to find me for the rest of the day became too upsetting. It began to undermine my whole personality. You know?"

He turned those spotlight blue eyes onto Tony.

Tony shook his head in total understanding of what Charles said. That surprised me too.

Maybe Tony wasn't the mental midget I thought he was. Turns out, he's Tony, buddy for life. I witnessed a moment between the two of them that I rarely get to see. I understood from that exchange why Tony was always around. For me, too, their exchange gave me more insight into who Charles is.

After Tony left, we went to bed. Now I am up because of what happened in the bedroom. Not the sex part, but the questions Charles asked me.

He had two requests as he held me in his arms after we made love. The first one was if I would go with him to Washington, DC for an anti-war march in the middle of November. The second question was would I please come with him to his parents' house for Thanksgiving.

The last request made more sense to me than the first one. But both requests made me roll over and away from him. Not because I was angry as he thought at first but because I fell into a hole at that moment that I hadn't known I wanted to fall into.

When I listened to him talking with Tony, part of me wondered where I fit into his life. I didn't yet have the courage to ask that question. Now there was an answer to the question I couldn't ask.

Mr. Charles Foster Payne became a much

larger presence to me as we talked in bed. His size didn't increase so much as his importance in my life now emerged to be greater than I had known. I felt tricked into loving him and told him so.

I screamed at him, "You've tricked me into loving you! You've made me need to be here with you. I know you CFP. You are a magician, aren't you? It doesn't matter what effect you have on my equilibrium, does it?"

He thought I was joking, play acting to show him how pleased I was. I let him think that.

I don't know why I should go with him to the march. Why would his family be interested in meeting me?

I write to my parents every week, but I never mention Charles. How could his parents know about me?

How can we stay with his parents, at their house? Then they'll know that we sleep together, won't they?

I can't believe this is happening. It's too fast.

I told him finally that I needed time to decide if I could go to DC or New York City. I've never been to either place before.

I don't know what to do. Why is this so difficult? It is keeping me up most of the night while he sleeps without a care in the world.

Today I skipped classes for the first time in my entire life. I can't believe all the things that happened during this one day.

I met someone new. I found out things about the Town that I never knew. We, at the College, live comfortably and lack for nothing, while just down the hill from the College, not that far away, live many, many people with much less. Thinking through all that I saw today, I want to become a part of the Town. I've been given so much. It hurts to see people who didn't have this same chance and who live right here.

Charles didn't wake me this morning. He left and when I heard the sound of his Jeep taking off without me, I decided to skip the day at school and find out where I live. I thought I would spend the entire time thinking about all that happened last night but instead I forgot all about it as I went about the Town investigating.

I stopped at a cafe on the main street and had coffee and lunch. I'd never been in the cafe before. It had high ceilings, it flooded with light, the tables were mostly filled with students drinking coffee and reading. I didn't read the Woolf book I had with me. I stared around the room like a character in a play who has awakened in a new town. The walls looked covered with large scraps of paper until I realized this wasn't some odd decorating idea but were notices, filling up much of the available space, even on the walls in the bathroom. I read some of them. The postings were by people looking for part-time work, who were baby sitters, cleaners, or they sold wood, could clean stoves, had hay for sale. None of this was part of my world in Skokie. I made note of it though and wanted to think about it later.

In my pocket, I had the $20 bill Goldie sends me each month. I felt like Virginia Woolf. In her book she describes what it felt like to be able to take herself to lunch after her morning's work in the British Museum. How she didn't have to scrimp on herself knowing that the money she had gotten from an aunt would allow her this kind of luxury for the rest of her life. I, too, had some of that richness in my life, not quite to the same extent. Goldie's $20 bill came each month and that was helpful.

After paying for my lunch, the thought of going back to the College didn't agree with me. I wanted to wander through the Town, to observe more of this place that exists at the bottom of the hill and that has been here much longer, so I learned, than the College. It isn't very big, this Town, and as the old joke goes, if you blink, you will miss it.

I turned towards the big white church we always passed as we came into Town from the College. For some reason it always looks blindingly white to me as if they painted it every day in that boldly bright color. Next to the church is a cemetery. I am going to wander through it on a day that is less sunny and colored by the rich harvest of changing leaves.

I walked away from the church and towards the town square. Old people and pigeons sat on the benches. The quiet of the humans was punctuated by the cooing of the pigeons who encouraged the old ones to throw bread crumbs on the ground for their lunch. The cobblestones around the square were littered with pigeon droppings and the uneaten bread crumbs.

There are no traffic lights in the Town. Traffic is sparse. What I saw driving through were mostly pickup trucks, loaded down with supplies or wood or equipment, covered in mud, held together with chewing gum and paper clips as Pops would say.

Not much seemed to be happening. I walked from one end of the Town towards the other end.

As I strolled along the sidewalks got narrower and then disappeared. On each side of the road, small, wooden houses painted in many colors sat very close to the road, too close, in my opinion.

We haven't had rain in a long time and the sidewalks were covered with dust. The Town had this quiet hush over it as if everyone was either taking a nap or had left Town for good. It was that kind of quiet.

At the furthest end, beyond the sidewalk, I

heard much shouting. I picked up my pace and discovered a yard full of children playing, screaming.

The children were streaming out of a solidly built, small house. They came spilling out and spilling out, without end. They made me laugh. Two women, one young and one obviously much older, came towards me along with their charges when I approached the fence holding the children in.

I think the expression might be that they looked like they were trying to herd cats.

The younger woman came right up to the fence to greet me. She held out her hand and said, "I'm Lauren," she said. "This is the Day Care Center. Would you like to come in?"

If they were casting a movie, Lauren would be the one they cast as "the Hippie." She wore men's coveralls. Her long blonde hair was tied into a braid that went all the way down her back right to the bottom of her spine. On her coveralls' strap a big red button read, "My name is Lauren. What's yours?" Her full mouth and heavy eyebrows made her look like she lived on a farm that grew children.

I hadn't intended to go inside the center but it turns out, she mistook me for someone who had an appointment to apply for a job there. I didn't care what the reasons were, I liked the energy of those kids.

Unlike how I generally feel when I am in a

new situation, I didn't feel self-conscious at all. I didn't question either Lauren or Elise's motives in asking me to come inside. I've never felt that free anywhere and I really liked it. Of course, I didn't realize they had been expecting someone else and this was a case of mistaken identity.

While I thought of Lauren as a hippie, my classmates at the College wouldn't have been so kind. To them, she would be a representative of the People. Meaning she is poor or at least much poorer than they are.

Lauren asked me my name. I said, "I'm called Scags."

"Interesting name," Lauren said and opened the gate to let me into the yard. She must have realized at that point that she had made a mistake. But she didn't seem flustered by it at all.

A large gaggle of little people now gathered around us. I couldn't get over how they smiled and smiled as if smiling were a constant activity. Not something you put on your face to show your feelings.

I looked down at them and asked this little boy who had been the boldest of them as he stood next to Lauren, "Hi there. How many of you are there?"

He looked at me as if I were speaking Greek. Another little boy came pushing close to me and answered with his fingers splayed in his face, "This many. And I am 3 years old."

He lowered his hands and waited for me to say something.

The other children waited too.

I answered by saying, "There seem to be a whole lot more of you than this one of me." I held up one finger. For some reason they found my raised finger funny and then as if a secret whistle had been blown, they ran off yelling and hollering all the way back to the sand box and swing set at the rear of the yard.

Lauren asked me to follow her inside the house.

The little school house had been built by the townspeople. Lauren told me the history of the grant writing and the design and the construction with a great deal of pride. The town needed a day care center and Lauren and Elise, the other woman at the day care, ran it.

The interior was just as I would have wanted it to be. Plants, fish tanks, gerbil cages, turtles in little pools, ant farms and the kids's artwork all over the walls. In the center of the room, their little desks and chairs sat in rows surrounded by mats on the floor and blankets and pillows that looked used but clean. A small kitchen in one corner of the space emitted baking smells. It looked as if they had just finished their lunches. A stack of dirty dishes sat in the sink.

Behind me, as I turned to take in how all the space was used, was a music corner. All their instruments and a record player sat neatly waiting for the kids to sit down and play a song or listen to a record.

The interior was really one large room broken up into areas that had specific purposes.

Lauren directed me to the "office." She sat down behind a metal desk that she had covered with huge stickers of flowers in crazy colors that flowers can't be.

"How did you hear about us?" Lauren asked me.

I must have looked away as I tried to understand the question because she asked me another one. "You did come here for the job? Right?"

She took a deep breath and the temperature in the room changed. From warm and inviting it was now at that place where each person wonders what is really going on and why you are sitting with each other. It was indeed a case of mistaken identity.

"I just happened upon the school. I didn't come here to apply for a job. I presume that's what you thought? "

The silence filled the entire space. I didn't know what to say, so I said the first thing that came into my head, "But… here I am and if you have a job I could do, well, why not?"

"Are you serious? It's a huge responsibility to work with children. It's not like getting a job in a library where you put books on a shelf. It takes patience and understanding to work well with little kids. They have so many things on their minds." Lauren looked at me as if I would understand her.

"Like what?"

She laughed at me as if I couldn't be serious.

"What are they thinking about? I would like to know."

I looked her in the eyes. Her big green eyes tried to factor in my knowledge versus my total inexperience with children to see if it was worth her time to explain to me what they thought about.

"I know what you're thinking. You think I couldn't possibly be the right person for the job. By the way, I don't know what the job is. But I'm curious and maybe it wasn't an accident that I walked in here."

Still Lauren was thinking. I couldn't wait any longer.

"I'll leave," I said, "and let you get back to work. Thanks." I stood up.

"Why don't you come back tomorrow afternoon around 4 and see what it's like here? Maybe we're getting off on the wrong foot. Let's try again when you are coming for a job interview. Does that sound like a good offer? Oh, by the way, I don't know if you know this, but the College offers credit for this job. So, you can earn a little and I mean a little pocket money and credits as well."

"What is the job?" I still had no idea. "How did you know that I went to the College?"

She looked at me as if to say, even Helen Keller could see that much.

"We need a tutor for our after school program."

We said good bye and I promised to return tomorrow.

I walked back to Charles' apartment. Everything that happened today was due to me skipping classes and going for a walk. How odd life can be.

I'm imprisoned in the library for the weekend. I'm working on my paper for Dr. Fish's class. I chose to write on the Coleridge poem, "Frost at Midnight."

The day has been gray and nasty. Perfect weather for a long stay in the library.

If I don't waste the time by writing in my diary, I should be able to complete my paper. How can I complain after all? I have such a fantastic life and so much to look forward to. I'm going to write in here in little bursts of freedom from work. Otherwise, I will waste this precious time.

(later)

Yesterday was a gray day too. I went back for my interview and then began work immediately.

(It's nice having my diary next to me. Whenever I'm bored or need to think, I turn to it, write something down and get it out of my mind so I can focus better on my paper.)

My first tutee is Jason, a 5th grader, about the size of a 1st grader. We worked on his math homework. Lauren said her form of interviewing is to watch me working with a child. So she sat nearby while Jason and I tried to get to know each other while getting some work done.

Jason's rather shy, mostly because he is so small, I imagine. He has a brilliant smile that when he trusted me enough to put it on his face made everything around him look much brighter. One of his treasures, as he calls it, is his imaginary trumpet. We made up a game to help him learn his multiplication tables. I play in an imaginary rhythm section. The challenge is for him to answer the math question on the correct beat. When he gets five correct, he can play his pretend trumpet and march around the room blowing out his favorite tune, which only he can hear.

That was my first day at work. I made the team. I now will work with Jason after school. I walked back to Charles' apartment and for some reason didn't tell him about the job or how good it made me feel. I didn't even write about it in here until right now.

(Later)

I love working in the library and playing my games. Today's game involved me randomly pulling a book from the shelves and then finding something inside it that had a message just for me. This game is called, let the library book tell your fortune. So easy to play, all it takes is a library card.

I walked into the stacks and pulled down a book. I cheat a bit and find a book title that is worth the game. It has to make me curious and excited to be exploring between its covers. The game is supposed to feel as suspenseful as any game of chance would. I'm supposed to feel as if my life could change based on the outcome.

I found something that made me laugh the

way I laugh in a library—that behind the hand clamped to my mouth so no sound escapes laugh:

> *and I am perpetually waiting*
> *for the fleeing lovers on the Grecian Urn*
> *to catch each other up at last*
> *and embrace*

Two things made this book a winner for me—its title, "A Coney Island of the Mind"—and those lines that made me think of Keats. It didn't hurt that the author's name was Ferlinghetti. What a great name that is.

I don't know anything about Coney Island but the sound of the words were so playful that I had to pull it off the shelf. When we read Keats I didn't think about about the particulars of those two figures on the vase. It never occurred to me they were lovers or that they might be running any-where. I never saw them in my mind at all. What always captured my attention were the lines about truth and beauty. I was seduced by the abstract nouns. They said, "Baby if you don't understand what we mean, don't bother with anything else."

The game is helpful. I see I'm having a similar problem in my paper.

I'm having trouble with one section. A similar kind of problem. One of those spots where the poem says things so much better than I could ever say it.

I feel like such an "idjit" when I can't think of a way to paraphrase what the writer has written. This isn't a stop sign but a train wreck.

(later)

I went outside to clear my head and to read the poem out loud. The trees heard me go over and over the poem as if I had lost something in it.

The light was going fast. Like the leaves, it diminishes quickly. The crunch of the dead leaves on the ground below our hovering library sounds as rich as the words pouring out of the Coleridge poem. The whole poem is rich.

Taking it apart to explain how it has affected me is really the point of this paper. Somehow I have to be able to explain why this final stanza takes my breath away:

> *Therefore all seasons shall be sweet to thee,*
> *Whether the summer clothe the general earth*
> *With greenness, or the redbreast sit and sing*
> *Betwixt the tufts of snow on the bare branch*
> *Of mossy apple-tree, while the nigh thatch*
> *Smokes in the sun-thaw; whether the eave-drops fall*
> *Heard only in the trances of the blast,*
> *Or if the secret ministry of frost*

Shall hang them up in silent icicles,
Quietly shining to the quiet Moon.

To have spent the whole night with Coleridge as he muses on his life's experiences while worrying over his young son's crib was a unique experience. The night went on and on for me too as I tried to figure out what was going on in this poem. I felt like Coleridge was telling himself a ghost story. His past sounds like that kind of tale—cramped, unhappy, waiting for someone to rescue him. Then he ends with a prayer that his son's life won't be like his. He will grow up in the countryside where circumstances will be richer and better.

I can dive back into my work now because I have recovered my passion for this poem.

[later]

I took a longer break to go for a run. My head cleared up but now I'm tired. I know what that means. Time to force myself to work, because this is the best time to work. Work will come out of me as if I am in a dream. Insights will appear that won't come to me any other way. It's okay if I actually fall asleep. Something gets released in sleep. It tears down walls that stand in the way of me seeing more clearly the problems I have to solve.

I could never make Mama understand how this works. She would come into my room and find me asleep at my desk. She'd close my books and pull my pen out of my hand. I'd wake up, screaming at her to go away and leave me alone, I was thinking. Later, I apologized. She never got it or why it was such an important part of my study routine.

[later]

I fell asleep and dreamed I had control of time. Not that I had the control levers but just had this ultimate ability to control its flow—to go backward and forward and to speed it up or slow it down. Also to go into the time frames of other people so that I knew what they were doing and when they were doing it so I could calibrate it to what I was doing at the same time. I have no idea why that dream got me so turned on, but it's a good thing Charles is away this weekend or I would be running out of here and all the way to his apartment to jump into bed with him.

Inside my head I hear wheels moving, gears shifting as if this were the sound of the rolling forward of the hours and the days and the seasons. The rolling wheels. Inside the wheels are corn and cotton and all the things we do with them. My dream was more like what Charles and Tony describe when they take acid.

I know that Coleridge was a drug addict and that Charles got kicked out of the College because of his drug use. I don't know what to think of it. I hated it when Pops drank too much but he drank too much because he was so unhappy.

I won't condemn Charles because I don't know why he takes drugs or why Tony does either. To me it is one of those mysteries that at first was just way too frightening because I saw what drinking did to Pops. When I fell in love with Charles, and in a way with Tony, it became harder to think about their drug use, so I don't think about it. I mean, even as silly and stupid as they are on drugs, they get their work done. Why should I worry?

I think I don't want to think about it. That's my answer to that question.

The sound of the wheels rolling though me means I must get back to work. My paper is already too long. Tonight when I revise it and type it, it'll come together in a shorter version because I hate typing. My plan worked. The paper will be on time.

[later]

Paper completed. Now all I have to do is wait for Charles to return. I can't wait. I feel like I did when we went on our first date.

I missed him, I really did.

Charles' return from his weekend in New York City set off a wave of jealousy in me. No matter how often he tells me he loves me, there is that spot inside me that is suspicious of him and everyone.

Truly, I am getting to know people better and to like them more. Even Kit, my neighbor is no longer such a thorn in my side. My roommate, Sylvie, is sweet, although we'll never be best friends like Eileen and I are. Lauren is special too.

But this jealousy rises up and makes me see the world in a blackness that makes all these people my enemy. If I can pinpoint a moment when the blackness returned it was when Charles began talking about his Halloween Party. He sat with me in the kitchen, smoking a joint and telling me about the previous parties. My jealousy boiled so high that it arrived in my throat. I had to put a frozen smile on my face. I watched Charles and said to myself, "He's having all the fun."

He jumped out of his chair and ran to the hall closet. He pulled out an old gorilla costume and put the head on.

"Tony wears this every year. He's the butler, hands out the drinks and the drugs, whatever the guest desires. He writes down the guest's name and the costume title. We vote at the end of the night for the best costume. I really love these parties, Scags, and now you'll be here with me."

He lunged for me with that stupid gorilla head on, trying to pick me up like he was King Kong. I refused to play along.

Charles asked me what was wrong.

"I'm thinking Charles."

He stood in front of me with his hands on his hips but with that stupid gorilla mask on and asked me about what.

"I'm thinking what I'm going to be."

He liked that answer and without playing with me more, he left me alone to conjure up the appropriate costume for his yearly Halloween Party.

On days like this, I think he has fallen in love with the person he wants me to be and not with who I am. That's probably typical with lovers. I don't know.

Where's my Aunt Money when I need her?

I'm going to write her a letter about this. I know she will laugh at me and maybe what I need is to hear someone laughing at how stupid all this is. She'll say, "Really Scags, just have some fun. Okay kiddo?"

Is that what she will say? I'm going to find out. I'm going to send her a letter tonight.

As far as Charles' party—I'm going to be my nice self and go along with all the plans. He will tell me what to do. I will do it, no matter what. He'll make his lists of things to get at the store and we will go together. Though, I heard him asking Tony to take me with him in the van. It holds more than his Jeep.

Tony laughed at him and said, "And it starts faster and doesn't stall at the most inconvenient moments. Really Charles, get the damn thing looked at will you?"

They drove to New York in Charles' car and had some problems somewhere with his car stalling out in unfortunate places. The two of them have been arguing about that since they returned. Guy talk.

Halloween is on a Friday night. We'll have the entire weekend after the party to clean up the apartment and for Charles to recover. I'll have my work completed for my classes through that following Tuesday. I'll have to make sure to give Jason his time too. I'll write to Aunt Money and tell her what a silly person I am and ask for advice.

This was a good day. A long day one too. I'm upset with Charles but I don't want to only write about that because so much good happened today that I want to keep that in mind.

So, Jason and I got along well today. In fact, I now believe we've broken through the new teacher syndrome. I found that very gratifying.

Like most Wednesdays, I ran the whole course with the men and women teams. I love the sound of the whole team out for a run—of our breathing, the placing of so many feet on the paths. It's an exciting sound, makes my blood race in time with my feet.

An early morning run like that is the best way to start the day. I feel invincible. As if nothing can go wrong in my life. When my body works that hard love comes pouring out of every pore. I know that no matter what happens, I will survive. Even if I don't like what is happening, I will be fine.

Alex set a faster pace than usual today. We all met the challenge and worked harder. When we finished, most of us were so "up" that we could have done anything we wanted to do—created world peace, found the cure for the common cold or cancer, been our own rocket to the moon.

The best part of running isn't the way my body looks but the way it feels. I'm often asked if I've read the short story, "The Loneliness of the Long Distance Runner."

The people who ask that question haven't read the story. It's obvious. The story isn't about what it's like to be a long distance runner. It's about something more substantial than that—about power and who has it and why.

I never could have written that down so clearly were it not for Charles. He has really helped me to understand this idea of class warfare much better than I ever saw it before.

After classes, I decided to do what Charles had assigned me to do for the party—buy the decorations. That meant I had to put my belongings together, leave them in his Jeep and hot foot it to Town to tutor Jason before shopping. Then get to his place for dinner.

I couldn't help but feel "Halloweeny" as I walked into Town from the College. The spooky sound of the acorns dropping onto the road, the wind tearing through the spindly branches, the sight of their long fingers scratching the sky made it feel very much like I had walked into a scary movie. By the time I reached the cemetery on the border of the Town, the scene was completely set. I rushed along; I still had a long way to go to get to the Day Care Center and then to the stores. I got so frightened by the cemetery though that the invincibility disappeared.

Jason was glad to see me. I think I smelled like the great outdoors when I walked inside. They keep it warm there and cozy for the kids. To me, it felt like I had walked into a furnace. Once we settled down to work, I forgot the temperature and the time. We had to buckle down because Jason was preparing for a test this Friday. I didn't want to rush him and I didn't want him to fail the test. I had created these puppets out of popsicle sticks for him to use as he studied. He had a much easier time learning when he had to teach the puppets how to multiply than he did when I tried to teach him.

By the time I left him, I was as certain he would pass that test.

I raced back towards Town and the stores. Now I feared the stores would be closed.

At least the Town is small and the stores close to each other. Partly because the College is an arts school, these stores are well stocked with all that I needed. But they are really expensive. I had a long detailed list from Charles. Lists by Charles aren't just lists of what to get but also what not to get. That's why they are long. And wonderfully written and helpful.

Having such a detailed list meant I got through shopping much more quickly than if he had left it up to me. I paid for everything with the money he encloses with his lists. I felt relieved that for the most part, I had finished everything I had to do before going to his place for dinner.

Suddenly, I felt light headed and nauseous.

As I tried to push open the door, I fell to one

knee. Lauren was in the store and saw me fall. I hadn't known what was going on but my body knew that I had done too much. Thank God for Lauren.

Lauren grabbed my arm and helped me pick up the spilled bags of supplies. She offered to take me to the cafe for a cup of coffee. I know I looked awful and could have used that coffee but decided to forego it and get home as fast as I could. I calculated how much time I had spent in my walks, the tutoring and the shopping and realized I needed to get home for dinner.

Charles wouldn't have been angry if I had been late. I wanted to get home and eat and lie down. I was wasted, I had spent it all today.

I asked Lauren to help me get home. She told me she would have to go back to the Day Care Center to get her car. I realized she didn't know I meant to Charles' apartment. I told her that I didn't mean the College but that I had a friend in Town and I was going there.

From the look on her face, it was clear she was confused. I would have explained it to her if I had had the energy but I knew complicated stories weren't possible at that moment.

In order to talk about something as she helped me to Charles' apartment, I asked her, "Have other students from the College tutored at the Day Care Center before?"

"Yes," she said, "and they really liked it. I think

they recognized that they were helping someone with way less than they had and it made them feel good. Though I don't think that's why you're doing it, is it?"

Her comments took me by surprise and since I couldn't come up with a smart reply, I told her the truth."I have no idea why I'm working there. I know I enjoy it and because I said I would, I'm there."

She chuckled, squeezed my arm and we kept trudging along.

"I don't usually buy supplies at that art store. They overcharge for the simple things I need. When we don't order enough through our normal supplier, I have to go to them. I wish they would give us a discount but I understand. They're in a tight financial spot. Without the students at the College, they'd be out of business as would most of the restaurants and cafes and other small businesses here."

I hadn't thought of that before—the relationship between the Town and the College. I wondered if Charles had. While I walked with Lauren, the cooler air revived me. That helped take some of my load off Lauren.

When we arrived at the back stairs that lead up to Charles' apartment, I smiled a thank you. And left her standing down there in the dark. My manners had left me along with all my energy. I should have invited her upstairs with me but I felt desperate for Charles and wanted to be alone with him. I ran up the stairs with all the packages.

I got inside the door and saw Charles in the kitchen. I left the packages by the door and threw myself into Charles' arms. He looked surprised at how glad I was to see him but not sorry about it.

I wish I knew Charles well enough to be able to predict what he will do or say. He's still a mystery to me, his wealth, the places he's been to, the things he knows about and has studied. Entering into his world has been like learning how to play in a completely new world where the rules are similar but not the same and people speak the same language but often mean very different things.

I wanted when I returned from the store to make us dinner but he had already made it. Everything was ready. We sat down immediately. I was starving. I also enjoyed how domestic our lives together had become. Something inside me wanted to blurt out the whole story about tutoring Jason. Put on a song and dance rendition of meeting Lauren and all the kids and then having been mistaken for someone coming for a job and then getting the job and working with Jason and his imaginary trumpet. All of that seemed like good material to set to music.

However, something told me that Charles

wasn't the sort of person who enjoyed song and dance routines. Pops would have loved it. Charles, I fear, not so much.

Having lost that one form of storytelling, I lost all ideas about how best to present it to him and so blurted out this confusing, silly and ridiculous account of something that I happen to care about very much.

It lit something in him and he went off like an angry man whose wife had cheated on him without first explaining to her husband why she was dissatisfied. I wasn't dissatisfied. I wasn't accusing him of anything.

On one count, he was correct. I never told him about it from the start. I didn't because, as I see it now, he wouldn't have agreed with me that it was something I had to do. When it came to me running in competitions with the cross country team, he had objected and I had listened to him and followed his wishes. Not because I didn't want to compete, I did, but because I knew about the time commitment, he was right and I wouldn't have been able, for example, to go to the march in Washington or home with him for Thanksgiving.

The tutoring job, to me, is completely different. But perhaps not different enough for me to have told him about it from the start.

As we argued, for that is precisely what we

were doing, we cleaned the apartment. I don't know how we figured out how to use the energy this way but for a while now, whenever we disagree, we clean together.

By the time everything was dusted, arranged and put away, the argument hadn't been settled. He thought I should quit and that I didn't need the money or to take the time away from my own work to tend to the needs of some little kid who wouldn't be able to rise out of the poverty he was in because some "nice girl from the College took pity on him and taught him his multiplication tables."

At some point, my work ethic saved me from continuing the argument. I bit my tongue and went to the now clean living room and sat down on the couch to work and to sleep. He continued to "explain" to me how using my guilt to help someone was doing, perhaps, the right thing but for all the wrong reasons and it was sure to blow up in my face.

He continued talking but I wasn't listening. At times I think he's not talking to me at all but to someone else he had a relationship with and she is making him miserable while I am doing absolutely nothing. Is it like this with most couples? Does one live in a battle with some phantom girlfriend while the current girlfriend battles her old boyfriend? I don't know how you could prove that but it might be interesting to know what it's like to live in the present and the past at once.

Maybe that is why young people are encouraged to be virgins when they marry. Too late for me.

Mr. Charles Foster Payne, I could have said to Charles while he complained about me not taking him into account, I don't feel guilty about this job. I didn't take the job out of guilt.

He finished arguing and went off to bed. I continued studying until I fell asleep on the couch with my books open on my chest.

At some point during the night, Charles woke me up to tell me he was sorry. I might have been dreaming except that he took me back to bed where I woke up a while ago and now sit next to the sleeping Charles while writing in here.

I heard him say the things I feel too. "I think I got jealous. I thought of you with that kid. You're spending time with someone I don't know. But you care about him. It hurt."

He held me close to him and we fell asleep that way.

The sun is rising. A band of light crawls across our bed like a cat coming to wake us up. I am liking love more now.

Lately I live in two separate worlds. One world is that of the College. The other world is Lauren's Day Care Center. Somewhere in that gap between the way we live up at the College and the people in the Town have to live, there is a great injustice. All of it seems to be due to accidents of birth rather than some design or contest that proved who should have what.

How does Kit not see how absurd it is that she drives her car to classes? I mean who needs to drive a Bentley? With what that car costs we could feed all the kids at the Day Care Center for a year or more.

I was trying to explain it to Eileen and you know what? She understood completely. Of course she would. I should remember, that like me, she is here on scholarship and even though she's involved with Philip what's his name, she is, like me, more of the "people" than of the upper classes.

I hadn't realized either that I never told her about my work with Jason. I was running around the campus, overjoyed that he had passed his multiplication test, realizing how many more tests like that he had to pass in order to do something with his life when I met up with Eileen for coffee.

I tried to explain to her about living in these two separate worlds that never overlap. Eileen thought about it as I spoke and then asked if I thought she and Philip could help out at the Day Care Center?

I must have looked at her strangely because she pulled away from the table as if I had insulted her.

"I don't know why you have such a look on your face, Scags," she said, "it isn't as if you're the only one who can be interested in helping out down there."

"Of course not," I said, trying to put my thoughts in order. "You startled me. I hadn't expected that you two would be interested in tutoring."

"Why not? It isn't as if we're incapable of it."

She was right. I tried not to be too possessive of things and then I am. I had wanted this to be my own area of interest. I liked that I was the only one from the College there and thus could be away from here without having to go out of town.

I hadn't noticed but Prof. Keating sat near us and had been rather obviously listening to our talk because he picked up his sandwich and asked to join us at the table.

"I think that's great, Scags," he said. "Offering time to help is a great way to give back."

He was busy eating what looked like a never-ending sandwich. It was so large and filled so full that it kept escaping the bounds of his bread. He took great delight in pushing portions of it into his mouth and then chewing on it at great length. Why should a sandwich be this large and demand this much work, I asked myself. Like everything that Prof. Keating did, he did it in a large way was my answer.

He looked tired, I also thought to myself. Eileen was pleased that he had joined us and began talking about how she and Philip could also help out and that that would mean more children could be helped with their studies.

Prof. Keating continued with his sandwich. It finally looked like he just wanted company while he ate. Eileen glanced at her watch and realized she had a rehearsal and left me at the table with Prof. Keating.

"These semesters get longer and longer the more I teach," he said after Eileen left.

"I am tired of being here," he said to me and I thought, oh no, I don't want to hear this.

"I remember the excitement when I first arrived. My mind worked overtime with all the plans I had for teaching and the students seemed to eat it up. At least that's how I remember it. That they really loved the way I taught. That convinced me our love affair would go on forever."

I had no idea why he was telling me his story. Even when he assured me that he wasn't telling me any secrets, I was still confused.

"Don't worry, Scags," he said. "I'm not laying anything heavy on you for you to have to pretend you don't know.

"I'm just unhappy as a teacher. It makes me feel I'm a fraud. When I explain something to my students, I know, in my deepest soul, that they will never remember what I tell them. I have even stood there with my mouth moving and no words coming out, and I swear, they wrote down something. Very obedient children here."

I laughed at that. He did too. For the first time, it seemed, since I had met him, I saw him laugh spontaneously. He was very handsome when he laughed.

"Though I am thoroughly tired of the drug-induced idiocy they are capable of. I wonder when enough will be enough for them. Probably when someone dies from it. Or worse."

I couldn't imagine what would be worse.

He finished the sandwich, he cleaned up the mess he made eating it, and turning to me he said, "Sorry, the weather here, while beautiful as it usually is in the fall, is about to turn gray. Then it will stay that way all winter long. That's when the real craziness here begins."

He stood up, picked up his large satchel and looked down at me.

"We have a tradition of inviting any students who can't get away from the campus at Thanksgiving time over to our house for dinner. Consider yourself invited."

"Thank you Prof. Keating," I said, "I have an

invitation from my boyfriend to go home with him for the holiday."

He looked at me when I said that as if he couldn't imagine that I was involved with someone. It wasn't that he said anything but the way he looked at me then, as if there were more to me than he had known.

That is probably true of all the students he advises. We all are much more than he could possibly know.

I'm very upset. I've had one of the most horrible experiences of my life tonight. I'm going to need more than a shower and a long sleep to get over what happened. It wasn't just that Charles' stupid party was awful but that Philip, who offered to walk back with me when I couldn't take all the drugs and noise anymore, tried to rape me.

Damn, what's wrong with that guy? Eileen and I will never be the friends we were, thanks to him and his stupidity. From the way she looked at me from his car as she drove him back in that horrible storm, she won't ever believe my side of the story. The true side of the story.

Charles couldn't contain himself he was so excited that there was going to be this dreadful storm tonight. In his mind, the storm was for him, to help him create the perfect atmosphere for his annual scary party.

From the moment I arrived at Charles' apartment until the moment I decided to leave, I couldn't take what was going on in the place. No longer was it the quiet apartment where Charles and I sort of lived together. Now it was this smoke filled, loud and drug filled space transformed into more of a theater set than a living space. My spine became more and more rigid the longer I stayed. I refused after a while to even believe that these people were having fun. Inside me the voices of complaint and criticism kept telling me to leave.

They kept saying that I didn't belong there. After a long debate with myself, I decided to leave.

Why is this fun, I wanted to ask Charles? Charles was having too much fun for me to ask him to answer my question.

I wanted to be a part of his Halloween experience. I made a great costume, I thought. I didn't tell him what it was even though he kept bugging me to tell him. I made it myself. Now it's torn to shreds. Between the rain and Philip tearing at it, it can't be worn again.

It took me a long time to figure it out too. I wanted Charles to be proud of me. With some cardboard, I made a clerical collar. I painted my black T-shirt with a clock face—Father Time. I drew a watch on each wrist and hung a pocket watch out of my pants pocket. My black pants had lettering on them, one leg said minutes, the other seconds, so that when I walked by, I was time passing by. It was really great.

I enjoyed making it. I enjoyed wearing it too. I liked how Charles smiled at me when I walked in the door. He didn't put that much effort into his costume—he came as a beach bum. Tony wore the gorilla suit. Eileen and Philip came as Scarlet O'Hara and Rhett Butler. Kit and her boyfriend, Lewis, came as figures out of Salvador Dali paintings. There seemed to be this theme with the couples of coming as a matched pair, as in Sylvie and her friend Henri came as Campbell Soup cans. There were costumes in reference to books (Tom Sawyer) and in reference to movies (The Wizard of Oz) and in reference to things I had no clue to.

The cleverness wore thin. The Skokie inside of me was restless to get away and out of the madness. I knew it was raining but I didn't know how bad. It didn't matter. I needed to leave.

I became a human cannonball flying out the back door and down the steps. Philip came flying right behind me. I didn't care. I wanted to be back here as fast as I could go.

Philip may have been drunk or taken drugs. Whatever it was he ingested, that slobbering sack of meat became a huge drag on my hasty retreat. He couldn't walk without my help and then couldn't keep his hands to himself.

On top of that, he had to start with this stupid, whiny bullshit about being in love with me. What a piece of shit he is.

He is Eileen's boyfriend. I kept reminding him of that. I thought when I saw his car coming after us that she was coming to pick us up, that she was coming to my rescue. But seeing him hanging onto me, she drove off, towards the College and left us to continue on foot.

Philip saw her drive away too. "See," he said. "She doesn't love either one of us." Then he pushed me down on the rain-soaked road and tried to rip my clothes off.

The funny thing was, he was so out of it, he could barely make his hands work. I threw a punch at him, which knocked him off me and ran away, leaving him there in the road to figure out what he could do with himself.

As I got about three blocks away, Eileen came roaring back towards me. I tried to wave her down. She passed me and drove back towards where I had left Philip. A few minutes later, the two of them came racing in the rain back towards the College and of course left me alone to walk all the way home, in the rain, with my clothes falling off my body.

Well, be that way, is what I say. I won't tell anyone the damn secret that Philip Fairview tried to rape me or that he wanted me to believe that he loved me. I wouldn't do that to my friend, Eileen, no matter what.

I know this sounds really stupid. Charles is having fun without me. No one knows what Philip tried to do to me.

I wish someone would walk in the door and tell me they were sorry to hear what a bastard that Philip schmuck is and how they're going to make him pay for what he did to me.

I know that won't happen. It won't happen because no one will ever believe me. In the way that Philip talked to me, I understood what it means to feel the hatred of men towards women.

I wish I had another diary right now to write in that was more secret than this one. I'd like to say things I can't bring myself to put down on the page.

It's sickening because now Eileen and I won't be friends like we used to be. That makes things worse. I don't care that Charles doesn't like her. She is my best friend. I won't be able to go to our tree in the orchard again with her. I can't tell Eileen what happened because I know, she'll have to choose to believe Philip.

If I repeated what Philip said to me: "You know Scags, I've fallen for you in a big way." She'd haul off and slug me.

I should have let Philip fall in the road so a car could run over him. That would have taught him a lesson.

Yeah, death is a great teacher. He wanted to get his big fat hands all over me. I could have hurt him badly on the road and taken off.

I don't know why I didn't. In fact, I tried to protect him from himself.

I really want a different diary to write all this down in and then burn it.

Can you imagine what Charles would say if I ever told him what Philip did?

I have to stop thinking about Eileen's face as

she glared at me out the car window driving by with Philip beside her. I'm going to have to act as if nothing happened, because, really, nothing did. He sure did want to rape me but he couldn't. I fought him off and that is what I must remember.

The weirdest part of this whole story is this: When I got back to my room, there was a letter sitting prominently on my bed. Attached to it was a note from Kit saying that it had been put into her mailbox by mistake. It was from Aunt Money.

I couldn't read it right away. I was shaking so hard from the cold and wet. I stripped off all my clothes and threw them away. Then I marched into the shower room and stood under the hot water until the shaking stopped. There wasn't anyone around. It's Halloween and people are off at parties everywhere.

When I got out of the shower I looked at myself in the mirror. I looked a bit beaten up. I don't remember Philip hitting me but he obviously did. I also have some scratches on my breasts and a long thin scratch around my right hip bone.

When I returned from the shower room, I opened Aunt Money's letter. It wasn't at all what I had expected.

In part she wrote:

> *Scags darling, if I could have jumped*
> *on that train with you in September to*

go to the College I would have. I would have done it then and I would have loved to do it when I was your age. At your age, though, I made a huge mistake and got pregnant and had a baby. I put my baby up for adoption because Goldie and Boomer didn't want me to ruin my life. I've missed her every day of my life since then.

Don't be upset for me. Be you, the wonderful Scags you are.

> *love always,*
> *Aunt Money*

The gray weather Prof. Keating promised has arrived. The rain that came on Halloween ended but the clouds remained. They haven't left yet and I have a feeling they won't anytime soon. It can be dark and gloomy in Skokie this time of year, too. Here the gloom has seeped into everything, including the friendships.

Eileen came to my room last night, crying. I thought Philip had told her the truth of what happened on the walk back from the party. I don't know why I would think that, maybe wishful thinking.

I tried to tell her what had really happened. Then I tried to excuse his behavior to spare her. I suggested it was the drugs he took. Or that he had too much to drink. Then I realized she didn't want to know the truth. She wanted to believe it was all my fault.

This further assault on me made me do something I swore I wouldn't do—I showed Eileen the bruises on my breasts and hip. Eileen gasped. I thought that meant she believed me.

But Philip had already concocted another fabulous lie—that I had tried to rape him and that he had to fight me off. That was how I must have gotten the bruises, Eileen told me.

The thing is: I love Eileen. Philip tried to rape me. He may have been on drugs and not known exactly what he was doing, but I don't care.

Now I hate being here. I just hate it. I can't let Charles see these bruises. If he does, he will go after Philip, I know that and I don't want that to happen.

Being shut out of Eileen's world hurts already. I never knew how much of an anchor she had become.

She's so angry at me.

I could try to convince her of what really happened but I've developed a new kind of exhaustion. I'm tired all the time. Even seeing her so upset and crying like she was, I didn't have the energy to prove to her that Philip was lying to her.

No one has ever been that angry at me for something I didn't do.

She wouldn't listen to me. It's become his word against mine. Who would I believe if I were in her shoes?

The point is, why would I want to steal Philip from her? She just assumed that was true. It goes to show, she doesn't know me at all.

How wrong she is and how blind she is. I hate this. I'll write her a note and tell her how I never liked Philip and so would never throw myself at him in the midst of a rainstorm on the wet road home from Charles' party.

How cruel of Philip to do this to me and Eileen. He's ruining our friendship because he doesn't

have the guts to own up to his mistake. I don't
know what to do with myself; I'm so upset.

I miss Eileen and want us to be friends like
we were.

Originally, Charles and I were to go to a lecture by this linguistics professor, Noam Chomsky. I promised him, I know. He's right when he says I'm breaking my promise. I have my reasons. One is, I never read the essay by Chomsky called, "The Role of the Intellectual."

I put off reading it until this past weekend. This past weekend I couldn't do much of anything. I've been so tired. I still am. I don't even go to Charles' apartment so I can sleep alone, I'm so tired.

I don't want to think about war right now either. Even though not going to hear Chomsky meant having another argument with Charles, I couldn't go. It's all too tiring. Why won't everyone leave me alone so I can sleep?

I saw a poster last week that Adrienne Rich was coming here to give a reading. I had discovered her poetry recently. I like it very much. Lauren and I were talking about her poetry. I mentioned that Rich would be reading at the College and not noticing that her reading and Chomsky's talk were on the same day, I invited Lauren to come with me to the reading. She got so excited. It made me feel that I was doing something for her for a change.

Having to then explain to Charles how I got confused took up so much energy that when after a couple of minutes he calmed down, I was just relieved. I have no energy to waste on anything right now.

I'm a slow learner when it comes to politics. I don't think it's because I don't care about what's going on in the world. I'm not angry at Charles for knowing more than I do. Or for pointing out that I wasn't even paying attention when the Democratic Convention was held in Chicago or how the South Side burned and rioted when Martin Luther King, Jr. was assassinated. I know my nose was in my books and I ignored everything else that was going on.

These conversations don't go well between us. He cares so much about what goes on in the world and talks about it with such passion that I end up feeling guilty.

I can't listen to him when he is carrying on like that. He makes me feel like a defendant at a trial who has caused all these terrible things to happen. Then I really can't concentrate on what he is talking about.

He asks me, Do you think war is necessary? My answer is: God only knows. When have I ever thought about that? There's the plain truth. I've never given it a moment's thought. Well, maybe when Dennis, a friend from grade school, began talking about going to college to avoid the draft, I thought, whew, thank God for being a girl and moved right along to my next class as if nothing had been said.

I felt invisible when any of these conversations

were going on. I remember when Kennedy was assassinated. I remember my math teacher, Mr. Katz, told us to write down on a piece of paper our thoughts right at that very moment. We had been in class when over the loudspeaker, Mr. Phillips, the principal, told us that Kennedy had been assassinated and that we were going home. Everything was going to close down and we wouldn't be back to school until after Thanksgiving.

While we waited for the school to let our parents know we were being sent home, Mr. Katz told us to write down everything we felt about that day. He told us that when we got home to seal it up in an envelope and put it somewhere to read years later. It would be like a time capsule. What was it like at that moment when we heard that the president had been shot?

I don't remember where I put that envelope. I see the blue envelope I put the sheet of ruled paper from my notebook into. I wrote the date on the front of the envelope and licked the glue, closed it and then put tape over the sides of the seal so that I would have to think twice before opening it.

Did Kennedy being shot change my life? It definitely was sad. I cried as I watched the funeral procession on TV with Mama and Pops. They did too. Pops smoked a cigar in "solidarity," he said with the president who also liked cigars. We bought Pops a rocking chair too.

Once we were back at school, I don't remember anyone mentioning it again. Or when his brother, Bobby, was killed, I don't remember much of that day at all. Certainly, I didn't grasp the significance of the King assassination either. I didn't even know that he had been in Memphis as Charles told me to support the sanitation workers or that he was planning a march to DC of poor people.

Charles yells at me: "Don't you see that in our times it has become okay to kill people whose ideas will change the way we live? That the real people in power now pay assassins to take out these guys?"

Maybe Charles thinks there is something I can do. But truthfully, he frightens me when he gets that excited.

Sometimes I believe that Charles has inside information about how the world works. That because his world is so different from mine that he knows things most of us can never know. That he can find out these things because he lives among the very rich and powerful.

I could write more about this but I am too tired.

I went to the poetry reading with Lauren. Charles went with Tony to hear Chomsky. I'm glad I heard a woman read her own work. It was so rich—hah, hah.

It also ended my exhaustion. Running didn't help me and sleep didn't help me but hearing Adrienne Rich read her poems, that cured me.

Listening to Rich read wasn't the same as hearing Lowell read. The power of a woman's voice reading her own work affected me in such a different way.

It was comparable to the part of "A Room of One's Own" when Woolf writes about that one sentence that made her start up and realize something revolutionary had occurred. It was the sentence that must seem to women now so commonplace, but here it is:

"Chloe liked Olivia."

When I read that sentence I didn't sit up and realize what had just occurred. However with the insight Woolf provided, it became to me too a touchstone of what has changed and in not that long a period of time.

So, tonight, sitting in that small lecture hall listening to Adrienne Rich read, was to me another one of those miracles, or revolutionary moments. In my life, I haven't ever heard a woman read her own poetry. I haven't ever studied women poets, except for a passing reference to Emily Dickinson who was represented as both an anomaly and a nut case. Her virginity being of more interest than her poetry.

Woolf shows the impact of that sentence in an historical way. I don't know enough about women's poetry or even Rich's poems to think this through that way. I wish I could. Instead, I have this observation: It's difficult to comprehend how radically changed women's lives are now. And how fast that transformation has come about.

Lauren and I had a long talk about the reading. It was through our talk that I could verbalize these new insights. It's as if this knowledge has been growing inside me like mushrooms under dead leaves. When I brushed the leaves aside, I discovered these incredible mushrooms that had grown in the dark soil inside me.

Now I see what Tony means when he calls certain awakenings radical conversions, meaning that someone goes through drastic changes at a phenomenal speed. This bubble-enclosed girl from Skokie becoming more engaged by and involved in the world. It has happened so quickly and yet, I don't think I know now any other way to live.

When Lauren and I talked after the reading, I recalled in explicit detail the way in which everyone in the room held her breath. As Rich read, no one uttered a word, cleared her throat or even breathed. The sense of anticipation for the words to come at us was so high that no one dared make a sound.

Woolf was blown away by Mary Carmichael writing that simple sentence: "Chloe liked Olivia."

I'm blown away by Rich reading these lines:
The refrigerator falls silent.
Then other things are audible;

There must be stages of involvement in a reading. As a group, we came together rather quickly. I can't recall the precise moment when I realized how attentive we were but I do know that the collaborative experience of listening to her words sent me into such an excited place that I think I finally understood what poetry is about.

The refrigerator falls silent.
Then other things are audible;

Now I understand as Woolf had—poetry isn't only written by men about things defined by men's lives.

I liked this line in the poem too:
this dull, sheet-metal mind rattling like
stage thunder.

This image made me feel just like I do when I listen to a solo piano piece, the way the notes go over my eardrums, as if I were the water skipping over stones in a river and enjoying that feeling so much that it is all I care about.

Lauren and I left the theater when the reading

was over and ironically walked towards the orchard. I didn't want to talk about what had happened on Halloween with anyone but realized, if there was one person I could trust to tell the story to, it was Lauren.

The nights are now cold and as we walked we left our breaths on the air. We turned back, to sit in her car and warm up.

We can be quiet or talk, it isn't important. I like how we each dove into our responses to the reading without demanding anything of the other. I don't know how long we sat in her car, but when I got out, a bubble rose above my head with the words, "This is the friend I have looked for all my life."

Mistakenly, I had thought Eileen would be that friend. Now I know it is Lauren.

How ironic that I learned tonight that Lauren is a singer and songwriter—like Eileen.

Lauren's self-taught. She told me a bit about her life. She's from the Town and has lived here almost all her life.

I asked her why she didn't want to leave and do what she was doing some place else.

She looked at me as if she asked herself that question all the time. You know, how a person laughs at the question before answering it?

"I left and came back. I wasn't meant to be anywhere else but here. I couldn't think straight when I was away from home. I couldn't sing the songs that make me happy when I was away. Some people are never meant to leave where they are from."

She looked sadly at me and then said she had to get home to let her dog out.

I told her that I was leaving soon for Washington, DC. That I was going on a march against the war and would miss a couple of days with Jason because of that. She just whispered to give her the dates before I left.

I got out of her car and watched as she drove down the long driveway hill and as her red back-lights disappeared into the darkness. I walked back to the dorm feeling that I had said something wrong. I'd hurt her but I don't know how. I thought I could be wrong and if she is hurt, I know she will tell me straight out. That's another thing I like about Lauren—how direct she can be.

By the time I returned to the dorm room, the tiredness had completely disappeared. I don't know how it could have evaporated like that, but I am not complaining.

My equilibrium has returned. It was a wise decision not to mention to Charles what had happened with Philip. Now Eileen and Philip have decided not to go with us to DC. Charles dislikes the two of them so this won't be upsetting to him. I'm relieved.

Oh God, I haven't felt this good before going to bed in too long a time.

We've stopped at a rest stop on our way to DC. We left early this morning and I've been sleeping almost the entire ride. Tony and Charles got the van ready to go while I slept at Charles' and made sandwiches for all of us. I'm sitting at a picnic table along the highway, gobbling down a sandwich, washing it down with some kind of Kool Aid they put in jugs for us and writing in my diary.

Riding in the back of the van is bone-rattling. I have no idea where we are. I'm happy to be on the road. It is a brand new experience for me to go off like this with friends. It doesn't matter to me at this moment where we are going or why. I really like being on the road.

Tony and Charles are meeting some people in Arlington, Virginia tonight. They have a training meeting there. So, we'll be stopping at a church for the night before driving into DC tomorrow.

Tony, who can be one of the most annoying people in the world, has this other side. He's one of the volunteer medics.

There's a new guy in the van I've never met before. Someone said he's a veteran. His name is Healey and he is quiet like me and watches more than he talks. I like him. He's very skinny, has his hair cut down to his scalp but has a long beard. He sits with no expression on his face but when he smiles, he is pretty, the way guys who are sweet look pretty too.

I'm glad that Kit decided not to come. I don't think we would have had room for all her necessary baggage. Eileen and Philip didn't come either and there are no words for how grateful I am.

There are three other guys in the van and one more woman, all of them are regulars at Charles' parties. Plus we have our bags and coats. It is a cold November.

Lunch break has ended. I wanted to get the story of this trip started and now I have.

I don't have the time or the quiet I need to write down what happened last night at the church. Getting a head start now is all I can do. I'll leave telling the full story until I return to the College. There will be so much more to write then as well.

I met this amazing priest, Father Jon, at the church last night. We sat up most of the night talking while I waited for Charles to return from his training. He and Tony had that meeting for the medics to attend. At first, I was pissed. I wanted to go with them and not be left at the church with people I don't really know. I probably behaved like a spoiled kid. Of course, by the time he returned, I'd had one of the most incredible experiences of my life. Isn't life like that?

We're in Georgetown now. People opened their homes to those of us from out of town. Tony found these people at the meeting last night and we will stay with them for the weekend.

I feel desperate to capture my talk with Father Jon because I know that so much more is about to happen and I don't want to lose what transpired between us.

Father Jon is the first priest I have ever met. In one brief moment though he was able to let me see what it is like to have your life built around your relationship to God. I've never thought about this before and it struck me so forcefully. Why? I don't know.

I've never been a religious person, ever. We never talked about religion at home in a serious way.

Oh shit, I have to go. We're leaving the apartment to go into DC.

I wish I could be back in Father Jon's church right now. Each time I think back on that night I spent talking to him, I realize what an influence he has had on me already.

I have changed many of my plans based on that one night.

The problem now is time. I have so much work to do to recover the time I spent in DC and not here taking care of my schoolwork. The work doesn't complete itself.

Where should I begin this story?

Being in Father Jon's church was almost like being in a library for me. However, it was also like I had begun to lay a foundation for something new to enter my life. It seems that his appearance in my life right now wasn't an accident. Something happened between us. Those things influenced what happened to me in DC. I know that something has deeply changed in me even if I don't have the words yet to say it.

In summary, I could say, it was all one hell of a trip.

Father Jon and I began our talk on this warmed rock in the church's garden. I was staring at the vast array of stars in the sky, not trying to count them but to acknowledge that there were more than I ever could count.

I wasn't really that rational. My reaction to the stars was as if they had grabbed my breath out of my chest and sucked it into the cold night air. It scared the shit out of me. For the first time, the word "universe" gave me the chills.

Father Jon appeared. He laid down next to me. We quietly watched the sky while all the questions and fears about life popped into my head. Father Jon could have been just resting after a long day but to me, he seemed to have been sent to answer those questions.

The first words he said to me were, "It's too cold to be outside, let's go in and have some hot chocolate."

Father Jon is this short, wiry older man with a scraggly beard and a double chin that sits right on top of his clerical collar. His left hand is deformed. He told me how it happened—he was a child on his grandparents' farm and it got caught in a shredder of some kind. It was a gruesome accident and they didn't think he'd live because he lost so much blood before they could get him to the doctor.

When Father Jon placed that deformed left hand on my shoulder, to guide me into the church, it didn't feel like a normal touch. He sent fire through me. That's the only way I can describe it. That bolt of warmth coming from his hand into my chilled body woke me up.

We entered the church and found everyone asleep in the pews. Father Jon and I walked to the front of the church and sat down in these regal chairs. We were the king and queen watching over our slumbering subjects.

I asked him if he'd ever been to a demonstration. I expected him to tell me stories meant to reassure my anxieties.

Instead, with his deformed hand he turned my face so I had to look him in the eyes. He asked me, "What is it you really want to know?"

My breath came right out of me again. I couldn't talk.

My eyes must have told him a great deal because he said, "Don't worry."

I have no idea why he chose those words but they did the trick. Worry, like some kind of unwanted guest, walked out the door.

With the loss of worry as my constant companion, I relaxed and enjoyed spending time with him.

He laughed at me. That didn't upset me. I wasn't worrying about anything. I laughed too.

"You must be hungry," he said.

"I am. And you promised me hot chocolate."

"Yes, I did. Follow me."

We got up from our thrones and walked back through the church and then down a short flight of stairs to a small kitchen.

A table was set for breakfast but we dug into it early. The room had an old-fashioned stove and a box refrigerator. A large kettle waited on the stove for Father Jon. He made us the hot cocoa. It was delicious and warm. We cut up the coffee cake and ate it. I felt full.

I asked him one question that then occupied the rest of the night. I asked him if the church allowed him to speak out against the war.

He took his time answering me. He slowly ate the cake and drank the cocoa. Me too but with my eyes on him.

"You are greedy, now, aren't you?" He finally asked me.

I burst out laughing and he did too. I knew exactly what he meant. Greedy to know things. Greedy to have the answers to all my questions. The smile on his face told me he understood me too well. I didn't care. I had stopped worrying.

He began to answer my question by talking about authority and why it moved people to behave in certain ways. He looked at me again and asked me how many times did I ask myself if it was okay to do what I was doing?

I couldn't quite figure out which thing I was supposed to not do that he meant. My mind ran right to the birth control, the sex, the sometimes drugs, there were other things too but he interrupted my thoughts.

"I don't mean you shouldn't do the things you ask about. I only mean that if you don't question why you do what you do especially when it is something those in charge tell you to do, well . . ."

He didn't finish that sentence.

"I get it," I said. "It doesn't matter to you what you are supposed to think or do about the war according to your church but what it is you think is right, right?"

"No," he said. He saw my confusion immediately.

I knew he wasn't giving me a quiz. There weren't any correct answers. The fact that I couldn't connect to what he said made me feel crazy.

"It isn't about what I think, but what I believe. Faith is a very different experience from logic. Out of faith, one begins to do, to act from what follows from that. Usually, not always, that isn't the most acceptable or practical course of action. Christ dying on the cross wasn't a very practical way out of his dilemma with the Jews or the Romans. It was done out of love of God and what God needed his only son to do."

At this point, Father Jon knew that I couldn't follow him.

I wish answers were as plentiful as my questions. I know it's going to take a few days to enter what happened in DC into this diary. I want more than that. I want a record of that time. I want more than that. I want to know why the two most important challenges to my thinking occurred there and what I am supposed to do about it.

I have so much work to catch up with. I promise, every day I will write down more of my story from DC.

I don't know if this is a direct result of the talk with Father Jon, but I need to record this so I can think this through as well. In my Philosophy class today, Prof. Loomis asked us how we learn to question things. In particular, he wanted us to think about how Louis, one of the students, doesn't let a day go by when he doesn't question whether the translations we have been given are correct. He asked us why we sat idly while Louis asked this question all the time. His eyes went around the table and looked at each of us. I watched as everyone sank down into their seat.

When his eyes met mine, I was frightened by what I saw in his eyes. He didn't like us very much.

His eyes said, how could you idiots sit here almost the entire term letting this bozo ask this same stupid question that eats up such precious time? He wanted us to shut Louis up. We sat like cattle, waiting for the question to be answered and then to move on to what the class was supposed to be about.

I turned to Louis and did what Prof. Loomis had pushed me to do. I said: "Louis, please stop asking this dumb question. I'm sorry that I needed Prof. Loomis to show me how dumb I am for letting you do this day after day. Now, I've been given permission to tell you to shut up. So please, keep that stupid question to yourself from now on."

I became an accomplice. Prof. Loomis got me to do his dirty work. I wanted to end the entire day that way—telling everyone to keep their stupid ideas to themselves unless it helped us all to understand what we were studying.

I know to Mama and Pops my "new" life is a typical rebellious outbreak like acne that will disappear soon leaving no signs that it was ever there. They see each period in my life as a phase I'm supposed to go through. At the end of each phase, they think I'll return to being the old Scags—only I won't and can't.

Since they have never taken a psychology class, they don't know you go through these phases in order to end at a new place, a more matured place.

I could show them an example of this idea of phases. I would ask them, what would have happened if Dorothy hadn't accepted that there's no place like home but decided to stay in Oz? After all Oz was in color and she had had all these new friends. What if she chose to stay in Oz rather than returning to that very drab Kansas and even drabber Auntie Em?

My parents would look at me and say, "But Scags, then there wouldn't be a 'Wizard of Oz,' that makes no sense."

To them, safety exists in the status quo.

When I asked Father Jon if Jesus was against the war, he asked me which war? I looked at him with such puzzlement that he had to laugh and apologize.

He asked me what I knew about Jesus. I told him the truth. I said I knew nothing about him as I wasn't raised a Christian but grew up with Jewish relatives.

"Do you know why Jesus was crucified?"

I didn't know the answer to that either.

"Are you interested in finding out why?" He looked at me as if there was no right answer.

His question bumped against me like something trying to push me off my course. It was a push towards something I don't know anything about. My first unspoken response was no. I didn't really want to know why he had been crucified. I didn't see how that had anything to do with me or my life.

If possible, I wanted at that moment to jump out of my skin and run around me so I could read what is written all over me. Then I could see how I've been marked by all the stuff I carry with me like a book bag crammed with notebooks of all my ideas and plans. My skin may be the pages on which I've scribbled every thought I've ever had. Maybe that was how Father Jon could read me so well.

I finally told him that I knew nothing about Jesus. I'd never been in a church before or spoken to a priest or even to a rabbi. We didn't have any religion in my house.

"Does Jesus' crucifixion have anything to do with war?" I asked Father Jon.

He put his arms around me and said, "Yes, it does but not exactly as we talk about war today. It has to do with the wars that go on inside our souls. When we can stop those wars, we will stop all wars."

He let go of me and looked into my eyes, "I know you want something more specific from me but hey, that's the whole truth right there."

I walked away from him then. Charles returned a few minutes later and bent down to kiss me as I put my head on the pew. I fell asleep so fast I don't remember falling asleep.

I'll come back to this tomorrow.

I'm not able to talk to anyone about the time in DC. I haven't seen Charles either since we returned. I'm sure he knows why. He doesn't seem to mind either. I haven't had the nerve to tell him that I'm not going home with him for Thanksgiving.

Trust is again an issue between us. What happened in DC that was worse than him reading my diary was this—I saw him and Tony shooting up while we were away. I can't begin to describe how disgusted and frightened it made me.

Why does he do drugs?

I know that everyone here does them. They are everywhere. People come to class stoned. Alex kicked two guys off the team for being on drugs. I heard while we were in DC some guy raced around the campus naked and yelling that the FBI had infiltrated the campus and they were going to kill him.

I had thought that being in love with me would help him and would be a great thing for me. Now it seems that I am falling in and out of love so quickly that it's more like a tennis match than a love affair.

Maybe I can't rid myself of Skokie enough to ever be in love with Charles fully. I wonder if I would have reacted differently if I had come here from Montreal or Brooklyn. I know Alex thinks Charles is too messed up for me to waste my time with.

I'm no saint. I too succumbed to the allure of

drugs. Though in my case, I am certain this will never happen again. I took some acid while we were away. The day of the march, everyone, me included, dropped some acid. I didn't get really trippy like the others did. I did it so I could be a part of the group, to feel involved with them. I don't ever want to do it again, but at least I know what it is like.

Maybe taking the acid was my way to try to leave Skokie forever. It kept me awake for a day and a half. The acid affected me more visually than any other way—what I saw appeared more intense, more vibrant, had more texture.

As soon as we arrived in DC, I walked away from the group and into the crowds. When I looked around, I couldn't find anyone I knew. I panicked and the panic intensified. I jumped when Healey appeared, tapping me on the shoulder to let me know he was close by. He became my shadow.

No matter where I went, he was nearby. I got trapped in a large group of singing and dancing hippies. No matter which way I turned, they did too. They wove themselves around me. I couldn't get free of them. Healey came to my rescue and spread the crowd away from me so I could move out of their orbit and follow whatever path I needed to be on. I couldn't stand still.

By walking, constantly walking, I could absorb what was going on around me, listen to the various speakers and not freak myself out by what I had done.

It was the stupidest thing I've ever done.

While I was tripping, ecstatic thoughts and images went off in my head. Not one of them remains as rich as it was then. One of those eruptions remains. It fills me every morning with its presence. I don't care. It can stay or it can go.

I know I behaved stupidly. Wandering around in that state, in the vast crowd of hundreds of thousands of people, wasn't the best way to take care of myself. At the time, it didn't seem so stupid. It was, after all, a peace march. We were into non-violence. I felt so safe, that had anyone come at me with a weapon, I would have walked right up to them and kissed them. That's how powerful the mood inside me was.

As the day progressed, that mood intensified. The drug didn't wear off for a long time, it kept getting stronger and stronger. The drug opened doors inside me that I hadn't even known were closed. Colors on that very gray day were so bright and vibrant, that I needed sunglasses. I was able to breathe exactly as Alex instructs us to do.

I had enough stamina to run around the perimeter of the entire demonstration at the Washington Monument. I wanted to carry a banner to help with the cause. I wanted to let all those people know that I loved them and would be their friend forever. That I would do anything they asked of me.

I know it all sounds so silly. Like I'm some stoned out hippy. It was wonderful to have no cares at all and to believe that I could live like that forever. It wasn't until the drug wore off and I felt the opposite of wonderful—sick to my soul— that I could for a few moments feel sympathy for Charles. Without the drug, I felt so awful, like I lived in a dark hole that had constant earthquakes. It never occurred to me that I was just in the van with its lousy shocks and inside a sick body coming down from a trip.

I didn't eat the entire way back. I sat in one spot and never moved. Healey sat next to me. His silence helped because sounds hurt my ears. The worst part was that I needed to be re-introduced to myself.

I guess in that Jefferson Airplane tradition, I had only taken the pill that makes you larger.

If I ever was going to take a drug again, I guess that would be it. I liked being 10 feet tall.

I must still be radiating that peace and love vibe from the march because Eileen smiled at me today. I guess we are friends again. I hope so. Though now we aren't the kind of friends I had wanted us to be. Her world revolves around Philip totally. We'll never be able to mention that night.

Now I am so concerned about the the war. How

incredible, right, for me to write that? It wasn't that long ago that I never gave it a thought. The news of the war was like some background noise in my parents' life. It didn't affect me.

The strange names of cities I had never known about or cared about. The numbers of those killed, wounded. The number of bombs dropped. The people who destroyed themselves to try to stop this war—all of that was as unknown to me as most of the names in the phone book and about as interesting.

Then I met a boy named Charles and that changed. On December 1 there will be a lottery, and depending on when his birthdate is drawn, it will determine whether he will go to war. I know I haven't written about that yet. I must. I have to understand it or I won't understand what he is going through.

Right now, the equilibrium is gone. I hope this is due to exhaustion and nothing else. I'm finished for the day.

I'm not good at keeping promises, even promises I make to myself. I wanted to go into great detail about every aspect of the march. But how do you describe arriving in a new country when you didn't know you left home?

I wanted to create a photo album of events:

> here I am in a panic, hoping no one asks me my name

> here I am watching all the couples holding hands and kissing and wondering where is Charles

> here I am listening to the music and dancing with people who want to change the world

> here I am when I finally realized how much I had been lied to

> here I am realizing that what I lived with was built on a set of lies

I don't know who made them up but I believed them, that's for sure.

I should have studied tonight but instead I read that Chomsky article Charles gave me a couple of weeks ago. Somethings in life are clearer to me now—It is time to revolt and change the world.

I have been brought to my knees with questions, doubts, anger and fear. I don't know shit about what goes on in the world. I thought everyone

I knew in Skokie wanted to live in that damn plastic bubble and I was different and was going to show them. But I live just like they live. Most of us live like that.

We watch the war on TV while eating our dinner. We sit glued to the tube while the newsreel runs and the bodies get blown up and the bombs fall and the people on the screen go screaming down the roads. They carry out the US dead. We watch and what the hell are we thinking?

What makes us, me so complacent?

You know we walked past the White House carrying signs with the names of the US dead and Nixon sat in front of his TV watching football. He knows we disagree with what he is doing but he doesn't care.

I want to do something but I don't know what to do.

Why did I go on this march? Was this some message from God for me to wake up and do something? If so, what?

I heard people preaching Dr. King's anti-war message. How black people were being unfairly used to fight it. When I heard a voice in the crowd that sounded like the voices of blacks from the South Side of Chicago, images exploded in my head, in black and white, of the riots in Chicago after Dr. King was assassinated. I remembered Julia saying that it served him right. That he deserved to die. I have no idea why she said that. We never talked politics.

I wandered down the streets of DC, the riots in Chicago playing in my head. Everyone was upset—the people who were caught in poverty, the police who had to stop the anarchy, those of us stuck up on the North Side who never knew that kind of poverty.

In that nightmare world, in the darkened night, I saw the yellow and red glows of the fires. I couldn't run from the chaos because it was happening in my mind. I felt the heat on my cheeks. It burned my eyebrows. The smoke filled my nostrils and went like a flash into my lungs and seared them.

All around me thousands and thousands of people already knew what I was just experiencing. They understood that these things happen and that people starve and are burned out of their homes and that they are killed or jailed and beaten up and robbed and that no one lifts a hand to help them because they are poor and black.

Voices that sounded like the people I knew in Skokie kept calling my name and warning me not to help them because if I gave them anything they would only want more and more.

I tried to scream those voices down. Tell them they are wrong. I reached out because I needed someone to steady me. I reached out and thought I had hold of Odessa and that she would pull me back into the real world. But it was Healey. He held onto me as the crowd marched and sang. I couldn't get those images out of my mind. The burning smell filled my nose. The heat on my face. He tried to let me go, but I grabbed onto him tighter.

He pulled me away from the crowd that I had pushed myself into, so I could breathe.

Healey's leather jacket felt cool against my skin. He smelled of cigarettes and coffee. The first normal smells I had smelled that day.

Maybe because I knew he wouldn't leave me, I finally let the whole experience come crashing into me.

I remember saying to him, "I don't care about war as much as I care about the South Side of Chicago. Do you know that it has been like a war zone down there too?"

He held me tighter and kept me warm because I think by then I was shivering. But I wasn't cold so much as angry.

Then, the anger opened a hole in the ground. The force of my newly known anger was so forceful it couldn't be held back and it opened the earth in front of me. Out of that hole a message for us all bubbled up. I was privileged to receive it.

I stood still at last. I stood in reverence of where the earth opened up and out of the burning hole came a voice and smoke that wasn't of burned buildings or anything man made—it came from something more awful.

It said, and I'm not making this up at all, I swear, it said—"Follow Jesus' teaching and love one another or you will all perish."

I'm sure this sounds like I had the typical hippy dippy acid trip.

I've heard Charles tell Tony that—"man you just had a weird trip, don't get all bent out of shape about it. It'll pass, wait for the next one—it'll be better."

I know how Tony felt when Charles talked to him like that. I know he wasn't pleased that Charles dismissed him like that. I know too why Charles had to do that. He loves Tony. He doesn't want to see him in pain. He can't stand it so every time something bad happens to Tony, Charles is there but he wants to destroy the pain and doesn't realize he's hurting Tony as well.

I'm going to repeat what happened to me.

The earth opened up at my feet. I'm certain that my anger caused that hole to open up, that voices came out of the ground with a message and then the earth sealed itself back up as if nothing had happened.

Out of the blue, something inexplicable has happened. It reminds me that I have things to do but what specifically they are, I don't know.

I have always known things in a rational way

and systematically gone about living my life. When I was told I needed a scholarship to get out of Skokie, I worked diligently to get it. I came here and wanted to learn things that weren't taught in the classroom—like what love is.

Now I am at an impasse. That's all I see.

I also know that once doors open, there's no way to close them again.

I took a long walk into Town today, but the long way around. I found a path that cuts through neighborhoods and keeps me off the highway. The dogs aren't too happy to see me. They don't frighten me. That is one of the major lessons of long distance running—don't be afraid of the dogs.

I wanted to see Lauren. Of all the people I know here, she seemed the best one to talk to. I don't know what to do about Charles. The image of Charles and Tony shooting up between the parked cars in DC haunts me. That scene has entered into the album of memories like when they wheeled Pops out of the house covered in his own blood. He tried to kill himself. I don't care that no one ever said those precise words; we all knew that was what he did.

Seeing Charles huddled with Tony, their faces waxed over from the drugs, they were like Pops trying to kill himself.

Why does Charles need to do this? Doesn't he know that he is playing Russian Roulette? This is such crazy behavior.

I talked a bit to Alex today about how things were changing in my body and how the changes affected my running. In his Alex way, he smiled at me and said, "Things don't stay the same forever, Scags, they change and then become the new normal. Don't worry. Just keep running. Okay?"

He sees simple answers to every problem.

By the time I got to the Day Care Center, I was so angry I wanted to pick a fight. I'm never like that. I wanted to yell at those kids to go home so I could talk to Lauren.

She must have seen how upset I was because when I walked in the door, she said, "Sit down. Cool off. I'll make you some tea."

She walked into the kitchen and put the kettle on the stove. She got the kids busy with their project and made us tea.

The steam felt good on my face and in my nose. I took a few deep breaths to slow down my heart which was racing like crazy.

She looked over the top of her cup and said, "I'm glad you're back." Then I remembered, I hadn't seen her since I returned from DC.

I felt like a selfish ass. I had barged in with no warning I was coming and no word from me in a week.

She has become that good friend I wanted. I know I blushed. I felt the redness on my cheeks and neck.

"We missed you. It's not often that someone from the College makes such a big impression on the kids so quickly. You were an instant success here."

I didn't know what to say. I liked feeling special.

She told me how they were using the stick puppets to teach the kids all kinds of things. I felt flattered to have made a contribution already.

After hearing that amount of praise, I didn't want to burden her with the story I had come to tell her. But having primed the pump, I couldn't stop myself. No one at the College wonders about what my life is really like, not even Charles, though he knows more than most people do.

With Lauren it all came flowing out like a gusher of information, probably more than she will ever remember. The children playing kept the noise level high enough that I had no fear they would hear what I said. Their chatter was a natural sound barrier. Once I got through the part where my father tried to kill himself, the rest was easier to tell.

She sat still and near me. I couldn't look her in the eyes. I couldn't let her reactions to what I was saying influence what was coming out of me.

I almost forgot that I had come to talk to her about Charles and his drug use. That part came out too. Then I could look her in the eye.

"Everyone in Town knows that the students use drugs. Because of their being users, the high school kids here have become involved in drugs too. At least that is what the parents want to believe."

"What do you think?" I asked her.

"I think it is more complicated than that. I think there isn't enough for the kids to do here so they need to find something. I hate the drag racing because that kills more of them than the drugs have. Going out in a blaze of glory seems truly stupid and a waste to me."

"Taking drugs is a waste too, don't you think?" I couldn't withhold telling her I had dropped acid.

She looked at me with concern but I assured her that was the first and the last of it. No more drugs for me. I mean it too.

I began crying again. I cried because I want things to work out between Charles and me but I don't know how to talk to him about that.

I said, "You don't know Charles but we don't have these kinds of conversations very well. I love him but can't be involved with a drug addict."

She patted my shoulder and stood up. She had to get back to the children and I had to walk over to Charles' and see if we could work this whole mess out.

That's where I am now. Waiting for Charles to get home. I hope I do this the right way and don't mess it up. What I realized while talking to Lauren is that I do love him and want him but not if he is going to do drugs. That seems simple enough, right?

Drugs and I aren't compatible. Charles and I don't see quite eye to eye on this issue but we are willing to talk more. We decided he should go home without me for Thanksgiving.

Some things shouldn't be messed up if one can help it, as Goldie reminds me. She called me the kid who always wanted to throw the baby out with the bath water. I suppose that's true.

Charles should go home without me. Then he can spend time thinking this through and choose if he wants to be with me or if he wants to use drugs. For now, I'm willing to wait for his answer. I mean it's just a few days and I certainly have enough work to do.

What struck me was that when we work at it, it's clear how much we love each other. It wasn't some schmaltzy scene out of the movies but a real talk. He was angry at himself. I was angry at him and at me. I never should have taken the acid.

If only all decisions were that simple. I am exhausted from all the talking and crying. He will leave tonight and I will see him when he returns. The draft lottery is on Monday. He comes back on Sunday. So much to think about too. I'll go to the Keatings for Thanksgiving. That's another one of those simple decisions.

My mind is beginning to calm down but this has been one of those weekends I wish I could have a chance to live again. Not because it was so great but because I made too many stupid decisions, enough to last me a life time, I fear.

Guys are the weirdest people. Either they don't like women at all or they don't know how to treat the ones they like. Or want to like and don't really know what to do with that feeling. Then there's us girls and our sensitivities. I know that what happened is my fault. I say I want one thing and then I do exactly the opposite thing.

I have felt almost from the first time I met him that Prof. Keating had a certain feeling for me. I never responded to him because either I was uncaring or I was involved with Charles.

Then Charles went away this long weekend and left me alone. Alone. And that set off a panic in me. I needed to be with someone and that someone turned out to be Prof. Keating.

I chose the worst possible person to hook up with. The man is maudlin and way too old for me. That's clear now but it wasn't clear when I decided to sleep with him.

I know, I know. I can hear it all rumbling through me like some kind of tumbling trio of boulders going off a cliff. I should have known how ill-advised that decision was.

It all began so good-naturedly. I had accepted

his invitation for dinner on Thanksgiving.

Sometimes I can't tell these stories right if I go after them head on. I have been sitting here for a long time now trying to find the words for what happened.

I didn't know when I went for the run on Thanksgiving morning how upset I was to be left behind. I promised myself that even though the campus was virtually empty, somehow I would find things to do that would keep me busy and interested. I promised myself I would have a good time this weekend.

The reward for that would be that things would work out between Charles and me. Next semester, I can go to his house and meet his parents. I didn't want to contemplate the other possibility and so what happened between me and Prof. Keating also caught me completely off guard.

The run was a disaster. I pulled my left hamstring. No one was here to help me work it out. The teams were away all weekend for competitions. I was injured and Alex wasn't here to help me. That one simple thing sent me into the worst slide I have had since getting off the train in September.

I came back to my room with great difficulty. I called Prof. Keating because I needed someone to at least get me some aspirin for the pain. I also didn't know if I could walk as far as his house for dinner.

He answered the phone and after listening to my story, he thought it would be better if he came and picked me up and that I stayed with them for the weekend. At that moment, I was so grateful. The pain was bad and the idea of hopping around trying to eat and get up and down the stairs frightened me. I had visions of me melting into my bed not to be found until Sylvie returned from Montreal on Sunday night.

Arriving as a knight in shining armor, because at that moment he was, Prof. Keating came to my dorm room. He saw the pain I was in. Took my small bag down the stairs and then came back to help me down the stairs and into his car.

I felt so grateful. I kept apologizing and then thanking him. I couldn't stop myself. It was that or burst into tears.

His car was comfy and warm. We went straight to his house and he helped me out of the car and into the house where Mrs. Keating while cooking away in the kitchen had warmed up a nice hot drink for me which she had left on the nightstand in the bedroom she had also prepared for me. The guest room had its own private bathroom. The bed was made, there were towels laid out. The bed was larger and cozier than my dorm bed. Prof. Keating encouraged me to lie down with the drink and let it do its magic for the pain. They would awaken me when dinner was ready.

I felt like I had gone from the depths of despair to the heights of victory. No longer alone in that dreary dorm building, I was now comfortably resting in a huge bed with all these pillows to sleep on, with and to elevate my leg.

The hot drink, whatever it was, went down like tasty medicine. It tasted good but smelled bad. However, it worked. I fell asleep and when I woke up, the pain was gone. Then the thought hit me that if the pain was gone, they might ask me to leave.

With the smells coming out of their kitchen filling up my room, I didn't want to have to return to the dorm and the food in the Commons for the next three days, sitting alone in a large room with this skeleton staff watching me finish my food so they could clean up and go home. I tried to adjust the level of pain I felt so that it was still severe enough that I couldn't be left alone but not so severe that they might take me to the hospital.

When Mrs. Keating came in to tell me that dinner was ready, I almost burst into tears again. She looked so angelic at that moment. Her hair had become a mass of curls from the heat in the kitchen. Her cheeks were bright red too but as I learned that was from the wine she drank while she cooked. She helped me stand up and even took a comb out of a drawer and ran it through my hair and asked me if I needed help getting to the bathroom. I assured her that for the time being, I was feeling much better.

I hobbled a bit more than I needed to into the dining room but it got me noticed and applauded for making it to dinner. The table was stacked with dishes and platters full of food. Around the table were so many new faces, it shocked me that I slept through all of their noise. I recognized their children, Jeff and Robin, from the get togethers Prof. Keating throws from time to time. There weren't any other students but a number of the Keatings' friends from New York were there. They all smiled at me as I limped to my place.

A Thanksgiving feast in the country began to work its magic on us all. There was more food than it seemed the table should be able to hold. I had never seen so much food on any table at one time. It could have been a wedding feast it was such an abundance of meats, salads, pies, puddings and breads not to mention the wines and beers.

I have never eaten as much as I did that night. I filled up like a balloon. I forgot to hobble but no one paid any attention to me. We got so drunk on the food that there was no room in anyone's mind to worry about a pulled hamstring. With no room for one more swallow of anything, I decided to stand up to see if the food would move down a bit so I wouldn't choke.

We left the overflowing table and retreated to

the library. I liked that room. That was where Prof. Keating had his meetings with us. It had a really nicely messy look as if someone thought through how to be tastefully messy. I sat down and tried to talk to their son, Jeff. He was too full to do more than groan a yes or no to my questions.

During dinner, Prof. Keating didn't talk to me at all. He was polite but mainly interested in making sure all the food was passed around the table and that we all had the opportunity to talk if we wanted to and that our glasses were full.

Mrs. Keating got drunker and drunker as we ate her food. At times I heard her make some comment about the "girl with the flowing red hair," but I sat too far away to hear what she was really saying. I sat between the two kids. They didn't talk but worked at eating the food. They seemed quite tired of all the adult chatter.

I suppose this was what a real Thanksgiving meal is like—too much food and drink. I wanted talk of fun things and table games and even some singing.

Instead I had to listen to Mrs. Keating talk incessantly about sex and make bawdy jokes. Prof. Keating didn't say a word, but their friends egged her on and found it all quite hilarious.

I couldn't listen. My face and neck got redder and redder as she went on and on. By the time we got up from the table and went into the library, he seemed ready to change not just rooms but houses.

Prof. Keating and Jeff and Robin and I sat down and tried to relax and loosen our clothes to help the food digest faster.

Jeff and Robin fell asleep immediately. The food did act like knock out drops. I turned to Prof. Keating and he was staring at me. I felt uncomfortable and was trying to figure out a gracious way to retire to that lovely guest room they had set aside for me. I picked up the local paper to try and figure out a strategy.

When I finished the article, I threw the paper down on their coffee table and tried to stand up to get to the bathroom. He saw me wobble and reached out his hands to steady me.

I made it out of the room and into the bathroom. I could have and should have just gone to bed. No one would have cared. But it seemed impolite after all the work Mrs. Keating had gone to. So, I decided to return to the library.

When I sat down, Mrs. Keating decided to join us. She doesn't walk into a room, she makes entrances. It felt like she had been waiting to do that—to interrupt whatever we were doing, which was nothing. She made a snide comment about how generous her husband was to the students while she and their kids waited patiently every night for him to come home for a home-cooked meal. And now, she emphasized that word, she had a gimpy kid to look after all weekend.

I had no idea that she didn't want me there. I heard her words and I stood up and left the room. I put my things together and straightened their room as neat as I had found it.

With that abrupt change in mood, I decided that food in the Commons was in fact preferable to what I had found in the Keating home. I said a fast good bye to them all, thanked them for their hospitality and left.

Prof. Keating jumped up and followed me out the door. The cooler air hit my face and I felt immediately better. I realized I had been holding my breath. He came to my side, offering to drive me back to the dorm. I let my guard down and gave in to the offer. I felt sorry for both of us. That was probably not the best way to handle this type of situation but I have learned another important lesson—having sex with someone because you feel sorry for them is a big mistake.

From inside his car, the world was beautiful, safe and quiet. The noise level at the table had been deafening.

Prof. Keating looked the strong, rugged type when he was with us. At home, he looked like a hen-pecked husband who can't do anything right. I asked him what had happened? Was she drunk? Another mistake in the long list of mistakes I made that night. Don't ask a married man what is wrong with his marriage. And never ask a married man why he decides to stay with his awful wife. There's no end to the reasons.

I have to remind myself that this little dalliance taught me many lessons, none of which I would have learned had I not spent the night with Prof. Keating

I know plenty of girls here who want to sleep with him. He walks like he sort of expects all women to want him. I wonder how many of them have seen what his wife is like?

It was when he cried while telling me one of about six reasons he can't leave his wife that I began, in my overfed and drunken state to take real pity on him. Clearly this man could use some holding and kissing and then one thing led to another and it ended badly.

Neither of us was all that comfortable in our bodies that night even with our clothes off. Too much food and drink spoiled things between us fast. I couldn't believe it. After all that sweetness between us, neither of us could really perform.

Knowing that Sylvie wouldn't return until Sunday, we pushed the two beds together and fell asleep in each other's arms.

When I woke up in the morning, he was gone. Can you believe that? It sure made my life simpler. I can't imagine what we would have said to each other waking up naked in bed.

For way too many reasons it was a mistake to sleep with him. All weekend the guilt has been rising. I am so frightened that Charles will find out.

My only barometer so far that no rumors of us sleeping together have leaked out is this: Eileen and Philip came back early. They got engaged. They're going to drop out of school and leave the country to work on some communal farm in Mexico. Eileen came to my room to show me her engagement ring. She never mentioned Prof. Keating or tried to poke around and ask leading questions. Nope. The secret so far is safe with me.

I can only pray it stays there.

The die has been cast. Such a banal statement for such a huge change. The lottery was tonight. Charles's birthdate was the first one drawn and as fate would have it, Tony's was the second. Can you believe it? The silence in our apartment was so uncomfortable that I felt like doing something so outrageously insensitive that it was all I could do not to.

I felt so many things about his fate, and mine, after the drawing that I almost disappeared inside myself never to return again. Never before have I had these thoughts, but I thought, it's my fault. I never should have slept with Prof. Keating. I should have told Charles about what Philip did to me. I shouldn't have stolen the book and on and on. Every transgression I committed said to me, this is your fault, you could have saved him, if only … If only I had known that I could, perhaps, have saved him, I would have tried.

No one can imagine the gloom that settled over us. We didn't ship Tony off tonight either. After the non-reveling ended, we asked him to stay and he did, and he curled up with us in the big bed in our bedroom.

Charles slept between us, as was his proper place. We all held hands. And stared at the ceiling. Numbness set in. We weren't quiet but mute. We breathed and our stomachs may have needed food but we had no appetite.

We each talked about our day before the drawing.

Tony went first. He told us of his run in with one of his professors about a late paper. He successfully got her to extend the deadline until this Friday.

"But you have to wonder what the point of that will be, don't you? I mean, now, really, I'm screwed. I could shoot off my right hand, I guess. I know a guy who did that. The thing was, he was left handed but they didn't know that at the draft board, they gave him a 4-F and told him to go home. Another guy I know just popped puncture marks all over this arms and told them he was a drug addict. He took something, though, that a stupid buddy had given him to hide the drugs in his piss. So they didn't believe him. But they called the cops on him and he got busted for possession.

"Man, this system is so fucked. And rigged against us. Ain't no way, no how, I am off to that fucking war."

"I hear you," Charles said and squeezed my hand.

Charles isn't a talker so what he eventually said took some courage for him. I give him that and a lot of love as well. I do love him, despite how badly I reacted to what he said.

"I know no one cares right now for us guys that

have to go and fight one of the stupidest wars in history. But, to you two, I am really indebted. If you weren't here, I'd be killing myself and I mean it. I hate feeling like this too and I hate it because this is exactly the sort of feeling that makes me want to light up a joint or shoot up.

"Tony knows that about me. He's been a rock, you have man, and without you, for sure, when they threw me out of here for doing drugs, I would never have stayed alive to return and do well and meet this lovely woman who has been with me this term.

"I know I'm lucky in that way. But I do want to just pack it all in and say good bye to life right now."

I listened to the two of them and my heart sat in my chest. It seemed so silly to be in love and it seemed so silly not to be in love.

My current problems were infinitely less significant at that moment. So were my current successes. And so were the promises he had made to me before the drawing on television tonight.

It no longer seemed of any real interest now that he had decided to give up drugs completely. That he promised me we were going to work things out and stay together, at least that was what he wanted.

Maybe I'm just paranoid about these kinds of moments in life. I wanted so desperately to believe him, that we had a future together.

He returned very late last night. He came directly to my room, walked in and looked around as if he smelled something was up. He had come to drive me back to his apartment. I was relieved to see him and to be held in his arms. We lived through our love for each other in bed that night without words. Charles lit the candles around the bed and brought a bottle of wine. He made his declaration of a drug-free life and all in all, I woke up this morning believing myself to be the happiest person in the world and if not in the world at least at the College.

That feeling carried me right back into classes where even Dr. Fish looked happy today. Maybe it had to do, I thought, with some sort of sadistic pleasure he took in giving out bad grades. But that assessment changed quickly as I looked over the comments he had put on my paper; his "bad" comments were complimentary. He shocked all of us by how he walked into the classroom. He looked good. Then he announced he was going to congratulate a woman on her work. God damn but that woman was me. Can you believe it?

I think the earth had to be off its axis for him to make that concession. I worked so hard on my "Frost at Midnight" paper. I liked being told I had what it takes to write about poetry from him. I would have given him a big hug, but I knew that would be going a bit far for him to accept. He had gone as far as any of us could have imagined him capable of already.

Neal looked back at me and smiled. He had tears in his eyes. We all, I think, felt so touched by Dr. Fish's ability to accept my work, and others as well. I wasn't the only one to pass his high standards.

I learned so much working on that paper. I could write a paper for him about how much I learned working on it. I learned what it takes to be able to write about poetry. One of the things that helped was having heard live poets read from their work.

So that was the best news for today. In my pottery class, there had been some minor accidents in the room, so, again, we sat around and shared ideas about pottery as an art form and pottery as a commodity. I still basked in the glow of Dr. Fish's comments on my paper. I checked out, as it were, from that discussion.

My other classes had gone well too. The end of the term is a rather long drawn out process. Most of us were focused more on the lottery than on class. If I had been in charge I would have cancelled all classes for the day. Now I feel like canceling life for a while.

What a week this has been. I have stayed tight with Charles because I didn't want anything bad to happen to him. He was so incredibly depressed after that realization that he will be the first of those called up to fight in Vietnam. I still can't believe it.

Things got dark for a couple of days in ways I couldn't have predicted. He even went out and had all his hair shaved off his head. He brought me a lock of it. I put it in the diary, at the back of it, taped to the back cover. It's sweet, I think, to have that little token of him right here with me when I write. It's brown and wavy under the tape that holds it in place.

Once he did that, he seemed to start going in the other direction. He came back from the barber, I shouted, he laughed and rubbed his bald head and then we laughed. It was sort of like gallows humor, I think, but he was the Charles who laughs rather than that gloomy guy I had been keeping an eye on.

He called Tony up and had him come over and we made a huge dinner together, the three of us and found a rhythm in the kitchen. I stupidly tried to keep up with the guys and took one of the knives to help chop vegetables. They gave me the salad chore. I loved it, every minute of us goofing off and Tony making snide remarks about Charles looking more like a convict that a soldier.

I nicked my finger with the knife along the fingernail and it bled all over everything. I mean it really bled. I almost passed out from the sight of it. Charles too. Tony, the medic, which he really is, grabbed my hand and pulled me to the sink and told me to hold it under the cold water while he searched for a brown paper bag. The blood wouldn't stop. I yelled, that, "The blood is gushing all over me."

Charles had turned white and sat down. Tony pushed Charles's head between his knees and when he found the bag, wrapped a large piece of it around my finger and told me to sit down too. And not to take the paper off. It seems that it helps the blood to clot.

Tony turned out to be the savior of us all and the dinner.

We had a huge pasta dinner and I mean huge with lots of red sauce that came from our kitchen. Many, too many, jokes were made about the sauce and my blood.

I liked how rowdy we became. Charles stopped being a ghost and became a flamenco dancer, of all things. Mind you, there was no music for him to dance to. He got inspired, as he told us later.

Tony confirmed my finger had its proper clot. But I wasn't allowed to remove the paper or get it wet. I was thus exempt from all cooking and cleaning. I let the two of them take care of everything and serve me.

Inside me, I heard this voice saying, "See, it can still be fun. All that worry all week long and he has recovered. All will be well now."

I believed that voice and things got progressively better during the night.

The best was still to come but I didn't know it. We ate and drank and then in an extraordinary move that I had never seen Charles make before, he asked Tony to leave. And wonder of wonders, Tony picked himself up and left with a big hug for both of us. He didn't say one word. He left.

But Tony is a good friend.

Charles left the room and when he came back, he had a huge grin on his face. He sat down again at the table, next to me and took my hand, the one with the paper bag around my index finger and looked me in the eyes.

Those spotlight blue eyes were shining right at me with all their brilliance. I felt bathed by something outside of the apartment, greater than the two of us sitting next to each other.

I was so focused on this odd sensation that I almost missed what Charles said.

"I want to marry you. I want us to spend the rest of our lives together. Will you marry me?"

He smiled and cried. That was how I knew he meant it.

I fastened my eyes onto those blue eyes of his and through my own tears, I said yes. I said yes twice because I wanted to make sure he heard me.

I'm having trouble writing down what happened today. My diary, the place I go to tell my story, has become inadequate to the task. I am engaged.

Charles took a ring out of a box. The box looked old and it was. When he went home at Thanksgiving, he told his parents he was going to ask me to marry him.

"I told my mother after I told my father. He said good luck, as he does, he doesn't talk much either. When I told my mother, I also told her about the drugs. About how upset you had been and that you weren't sure you could stay with me anymore. She said she liked you for that. She loved you for that."

He took a deep breath. So did I.

"Then she went into her bedroom and came back with this box and the ring inside it which was her mother's engagement ring. I know, Scags, that this is somewhat corny and ridiculous but it meant so much to me that my mother handed this to me. In the past, she hid things from me so I wouldn't sell them for drugs."

We both stopped then. I've never been so moved by anything before. I haven't met his mother yet but I know when I do I am going to love her.

He held me as he told me the rest of the story.

"She told me to tell you that she wanted you to

have this ring. That she's sorry her mother isn't alive to be with us at our wedding."

He slipped the ring onto my finger and we sat looking at it on my hand. It fit. It gleamed in the lights over our messy kitchen table. On that ring finger, his world and mine were about to combine. I had to get rid of that mess on my index finger where I had cut myself, but Charles told me to wait. There was plenty of time to admire the ring.

I'm sure that everyone asks themselves if they are in a dream when something like this happens. I am asking myself that and telling myself if it is a dream, please don't wake me up. I'm too happy.

Today was my first day as an engaged person. I know that sounds really awkward. I haven't come up with a way to say it that is comfortable. Charles' fiance makes me uncomfortable, as if he now has taken formal possession of me.

In a way he has. Getting married obviously changes so many things, especially as they affect my plans for my life. Now when I think about it, it isn't solely mine when it comes to making plans.

Similar to but not the same, if I decide to take a job tutoring again, I do have to talk to Charles about it. It won't be to ask his permission but to inform him of it so that we can take that into account as we make plans. But what if he says things to me like, I don't want you to work.

I'm not going to think those thoughts now or ever.

What if he finds out what happened between me and Prof. Keating or between me and Philip? Again, I have instructed myself to no longer think about these two meaningless events. Not now, not ever.

Before any of those doubts or worries rose in me, I went for a short run this morning. The morning light woke me up. Charles was still asleep. He couldn't be budged from his spot on the bed, so I thought, why not take a quick run around Town to burn up some of this excess energy?

I left a note telling him where I had gone and that I would be back soon.

By the time I got outside, the sun's rays were grazing the tops of the mountains. I stretched out my bad leg before starting out. It was cold and I knew even with the sun making its full appearance there wouldn't be enough warmth from it to keep that muscle from cramping unless I really stretched. I hate stretching. But today, it felt good. I feel older now that I am engaged. My legs need to last me a long time. I was a silly person to think they would last me forever if I didn't take better care of them.

As I started out, slowly finding my pace, there were more thoughts. Thoughts such as this one: I'm only 18 years old. What the fuck am I doing? I've never slept, well, had a relationship with any other man. I've had no experiences to compare my love of Charles to.

I knew I was right. I also knew that was a good thought to begin a run with. I needed to be reminded of that because many people will wonder about it. I can hear my parents raised eyebrows. Yes, you can hear raised eyebrows.

Mama especially with those full eyebrows of hers, lifting them in wonder. How, she might ask, is it at this young age that you need to marry?

I ran and breathed and kept a good pace and in the midst of the run, as the questions and concerned piled in without stop, I didn't stop or stop them. I wanted all that concern to pile up or to fly at me and to pass it by with ease. In the midst of all the worries and concerns of others, the one thing that flew up and out of me as I ran, as right as the air and the skin covered with the sweat from my exertion was the fact, the glorious fact, that Charles and I loved each other.

I jumped over all those obstacles with ease. They loomed up and I didn't bolt when it came time to hurdling them; I was up and over with such room to spare that I gathered more of the concerns and made them rise up so that I could glide over them. Love and running go hand in hand.

I finished my run and remembered to stretch that leg again. When I climbed the stairs to come back indoors, I pulled off my gloves. There on my left hand sat a ring that had never been there before. It felt like an alien visitor. I hope that sensation disappears soon. Never having worn a ring, I am not sure why it feels like, I don't know, like a tooth that doesn't belong in my mouth would feel, I guess.

I'll make it happy to be there, I said to myself. I opened the door to the apartment. Sunlight flooded the kitchen but Charles wasn't in there like I had expected him to be. I raced into the bedroom to make sure that everything was okay.

Charles was sitting up in bed, drinking coffee and reading the newspapers. He looked so happy to see me. It's going to be nice to have that smile to look forward to every day.

"Sundays are family days," Charles said as he strode out of the shower this morning. I wasn't sure what he meant by that. I was still in bed, reading poetry, Adrienne Rich mostly but other books littered my side of the bed. He had a towel wrapped around his middle and with no hair on head, he looked different to me. More like someone from my side of the tracks than from his. I know we never talk about this. How rich he is but he is.

We spent Saturday night giggling through a number of the plans we want to make. With the winter break coming up, we will be off campus for a few weeks. Charles told me his parents have an apartment in Paris where we could go to plan what we want to do next.

He said, "My parents have an apartment in Paris," the way I would say, "My parents have a split-level house in Skokie."

Inside me, a little well began to fill up with these warm waters. Like the cold and emptiness I had anticipated in my return to Skokie during this upcoming break had disappeared. Now, I was in the midst of planning a trip to Paris.

However, before those plans could be put into place, Charles wanted to call my parents to tell them the news.

"Charles," I said, "don't you think I should get out of bed first and start my day before we try and call them? Besides, it's an hour earlier there."

I forgot to look at the clock; we had slept in and it was already noon.

"My point exaclty. Calling them before you have the chance to chicken out. Give me the number."

He stood at the foot of the bed. Fully dressed now and looking quite handsome in his heavy woolen shirt and blue jeans, he was ready to do anything. All hints of that devastating depression had lifted.

Seeing him so happy, I didn't want to refuse him anything. In all honesty, this was one of the more distasteful things he could have asked me to do.

I told him, but I was just joking, "I'd rather die first. You can bury me and then dig me up once they've had some time to think things through."

He didn't find my comment funny at all.

Charles reminded me that he'd already told his parents. He didn't see why I couldn't tell mine. I knew I couldn't put this off forever. Comments like, not all parents are made the same, weren't going to dissuade him, I could see that.

He went on to say that his parents were upset that I hadn't come with him as we had planned. His goading worked. I gave him their phone number and I could see by the smirk on his face that he felt like he had won a big moral victory.

He went into the living room to place the call. I would have preferred getting dressed, having breakfast, waiting a little longer.

He laughed at me and said, "They can't see you, so relax. These are your parents we're calling."

"I know'" I said, "that's the problem. You'll see."

He dialed their number and waited for someone to answer. I could tell by the look on his face that it was Odessa who answered the phone. She must have been surprised when he said who he was and that he needed to speak to my father. When she heard him ask to speak to my Pops, she wisely put Mama on the phone.

I watched Charles talk to my Mama. This was the first time in my life a man had called my family to tell them good news. He enjoyed talking to Mama, which must be a sign of good things to come.

I've never seen Charles look like he did talking to Mama about our future plans. As hazy as they are, he seemed at ease to admit we didn't know much yet. Or as he said it, "We haven't formalized them yet, but we are working on it."

He even promised to keep her up to date with what we were going to do. Then she started talking on her end. I never thought Mama could talk this much to a complete stranger. She made him laugh. He laughed a few times and when I asked him what it was, he turned his back to me and continued listening to Mama. They talked a long time and then he handed me the phone.

For some reason, I hadn't realized that I, too, would have to talk.

"Hello Mama," I said and heard her sigh with relief.

"Scags, I 'm so happy for you. He sounds so nice and smart. I can tell he likes you and that makes me happy. You can't tell much about a person talking to them on the telephone but I am glad he called. That was a very gentlemanly thing to do. How expensive is this call getting to be? Do you want me to call you back?"

I had to assure her that not only was it okay to talk as long as we wanted but not to worry. If she wanted to talk to us, she should call here collect.

Charles watched me as I talked to Mama. When I told her to call us whenever she wanted to but collect, he shook his head yes. His smile said to me that I had done a wonderful and brilliant thing. Why hadn't he thought of that? Being in love changes so much about how two people are with each other, I see now.

Mama whispered to me on the phone, "Is he rich, Scags?"

There was no reason to whisper back; Charles couldn't hear the question. I replied, "Yes he is fabulous Mama and I can't wait for you to meet him."

"Oh Scags," Mama said, "I am so happy for you. You will have a good life now, I know that. I'm going to figure out how to tell your Pops. I want him to know how grown up and ready to move along you are. I'm sure he will be happy too. Don't worry about that. Odessa has been standing here listening to us talk. Her smile will light up all of Chicago tonight, Scags. I love you."

Silence sometimes works as an answer between us. I took a deep breath and said I had to go.

"I know Scags. Take care."

We hung up.

I grabbed Charles and took him with me into the shower. We eventually ran out of hot water. What a crazy way to live, but I love being in love.

With each day, I pray that my finger will adjust better to the ring on it. It still feels like a foreign object that my hand wants to reject. I see no symbolic significance in this and as it turns out, when I had coffee with Eileen today, she reported the same problem with her ring.

Eileen saw the ring on my finger before I could tell her the news. We were in the Commons again. Her classes are basically over and she had some time to relax. Without Philip at her side, which is a rare event, I felt encouraged to sit down and talk. It felt like it used to feel when we didn't know Charles or Philip. We talked for a long time so I drank more coffee than I'm used to. I may never sleep again.

We sure could talk but the content of our conversation has changed. Eileen talks about raising animals and growing crops in Mexico. I tell her we're thinking about going to Paris during the winter break.

Eileen asked me sort of shyly if I was having any trouble adjusting to my ring. What a relief that was. I told her my finger wasn't happy with it but I was going to tough it out because I knew eventually I wouldn't even know it was there.

She looked at me as if I had saved her life.

"Philip wants me to believe that I don't want to marry him because the ring is uncomfortable. I remind him that I am giving up a career as a singer to follow him to Mexico so I don't think it's about my ambivalence. He taught me that word in the process of explaining to me why the ring was uncomfortable."

At that moment, I don't think Eileen wanted me to see the inner workings of her life with Philip but there it was. Already the two of them weren't getting along. I said not one word and let it all go by. Goldie would have been proud of me.

I guess, to resume some control over the conversation, Eileen said to me about my engagement, "I can't believe he proposed and you accepted. I mean, you two have, well, such completely different backgrounds not to mention study habits."

She may have wanted to jab at me but she was correct. We come from radically different backgrounds.

"Yes, true but the next semester won't really be that different from this one. Except that I will be living with him off campus." I left unsaid that neither she nor Philip would be on campus or in school and that she was throwing away a full scholarship to follow him to Mexico to be a farmer.

I don't think I like myself for having said that to her or even what I left unsaid. I got up and left. I mumbled something about an appointment I forgot I had.

As more people find out that Charles and I are engaged, the weirdest shit seems to happen. No one has no opinion about this new arrangement. Not even his old girl friends seem to want to keep their feelings to themselves. It makes for good story telling, though at the moment when Ivy burst into our bedroom, I didn't find it funny at all.

Ivy let herself into our apartment last night. We were lying in bed and she used her old key. She strutted through the apartment right into the bedroom, and plopped herself down on our bed as if we were old friends.

I don't think she knew how frightening it was to just burst into our apartment like that. Charles, for some reason, was completely calm. She stood in our bedroom and told us that we were sleeping in the same bed that she and Charles had slept in. She informed us that where she came from that wasn't done.

Charles told her, "Where I come from, people don't prance into someone's bedroom uninvited."

Then she looked at me and at Charles and said, "Of course it does depend what you are used to."

Charles had had enough of her and hopped out of the bed. He took Ivy by the arm and escorted her out of the room and then out of our apartment. I heard her make some comment about the fact that he was naked. I wanted to ask her what did she expect, we were in bed.

Charles had to pry the key from her fingers, but he came back to bed holding it up like a prize.

I asked him how many more girlfriends should we be expecting?

"News travels fast here. I suppose it's good we got engaged at the end of the term. We'll be old news by the time we return in February."

I suggested he make the rounds though and pick up all those old keys or change the locks. I didn't like lying in bed next to him and being insulted.

I also told him to wear his pants the next time he escorted anyone but me out of this room.

The only person I hadn't told yet who I wanted to tell in person was Lauren. I had kept to my regular tutoring schedule and thought at some point I would be able to talk to her. She's been sick for a few days and when I went to the Day Care Center today to work with Jason, Elise said she hadn't returned to work yet. I asked if it would be okay for me to pay her a visit after Jason and I finished his lesson.

Elise said she was sure Lauren would love to have company. She gave me the address and directions to find it. That was a good thing as I get lost easily in the dark here.

She reminded me to keep my distance from Lauren so as not to pick up her cold. I assured her I would be careful and then gave myself a huge pat on the back for having been around all these sniffling and coughing children and not getting sick.

I walked in the dark to Lauren's house following the directions carefully. There aren't many street lamps in Town and the sidewalks are narrow and uneven. I didn't want to fall on my way to her house.

When I arrived, I took a deep breath and walked up to her front door. I realized I should have brought tht her something for her cold. I knocked and she opened the door and looked startled to see me. I woke her up. I offered to leave. She begged me to come inside. She led me into her library at the back of the house. Her library was so warm and cozy and it felt like being in a temple devoted to books. Everywhere I looked they sat, spine out, face out, opened, marked with bookmarks. But treated with respect.

"It gets lonely being sick. I forgot. I rarely pick up these kids' cold anymore but when I do . . ."

She left her sentence unfinished as she is having trouble talking with the cold.

I sat down in a chair as far away from her as possible. Her dog came bounding out of the bedroom to be with us.

Lauren asked me why I looked so brilliantly happy. I loved that description. It made it easy to blurt out, "Charles proposed to me over the weekend." I showed her the ring as proof of his proposal.

She looked startled. I expected that. Also as I expected, I saw the but, but, buts . . . forming in her mind but she didn't say them. She smiled at me and said how happy she was for me.

She wanted to know when and where we were getting married. I told her that we hadn't decided yet. For now, we were going away at the end of the term. We wanted to rest and to be alone.

I couldn't believe these words keep coming out of my mouth about Charles' family having a place in Paris we might go to. It sounds foreign to me too that some place in a country I have never been to there is a house that I am free to go to with my future husband.

She laughed and put her hand out to her dog to keep her from bothering me. I didn't mind though.

She said, "You're set then? Life is going to be very different for you now, isn't it? Having a wealthy husband is a game changer as they say."

I looked at her as if I could see her words balloon up in the room. She said it. Now that Lauren has said that about the money, I know others are thinking that too. Charles is very wealthy and that will change my life immensely, I know that. How, at this moment, I'm not sure.

"Yes, he has money. But as old-fashioned as this sounds, if he lost it all right now, I'd still marry him."

"And I'm sure that's true but you're not going to have to worry about that right now. I am still sick, Scags. I hate to have to kick you out, but I must go back to bed."

I left Lauren's assuring her I wasn't going to catch her cold and that I was still going to work at the Day Care Center.

She laughed at me and said, "Of course you are but you're going to work for free."

I laughed too. I so like being with Lauren and I am going to be able to spend more time at the Day Care Center next term because my life will be much simpler.

As I closed her front door against the cold air, I heard her yell after me, "Congratulations, and you'd better invite me to the wedding."

I ran off and came back to Charles' place. I made a note in my head and now in here. No matter where we get married, Lauren will be there. I'll make sure of that.

Charles and I had one more person who is special to us to celebrate our engagement with and that was Tony. He was going to cook for us a feast at his place, where I had never been so we could sit for as long as we wanted and have fun, the three of us.

All week long he had been bothering Charles, asking him questions about foods I liked and didn't like. What wines went best with what he was cooking. He was in agony that this dinner be first class.

We were supposed to get started early in the evening because no matter what else may be happening in my life, I must run or everyone pays the consequences.

I was up here in my dorm room putting some things away for next term when Charles came racing up the stairs to ask me a question. I can't recall at this moment what it was. In the process of answering that question, he and I started talking about the winter recess and how we now certainly needed to make reservations if we were going anywhere at all.

I don't know why putting clothes away distracted me so much but it did. He wanted me to make a decision and I replied that I would leave it up to him but it dawned on me that I had had enough of the cold so why couldn't we go some place warm.

He laughed. He said, "I offer you Paris and you want Florida."

I could have killed him at that moment. "That was not what I meant by some place warm," I said. "I meant an island somewhere that is quiet and romantic. Why would I want to go to Florida?"

"I thought you all liked Florida in the winter. Isn't that why you don't want to go to Paris now?"

"What kind of dumb fuck question is that?" I looked at him as if he had just transformed from some kind of kind, innocent soul into the devil incarnate.

"Don't you talk to me like that," he said and walked out the door. "I'll be back to pick you up in an hour. If you're lucky."

He walked out and I threw the shoe that was in my hand at his retreating back.

That was the last I saw of him.

I never should have let him leave my room without finishing that argument and settling that he isn't anti-semitic and I'm not some Jew from Skokie who needs to be in Florida in the winter.

The fact that we will never see each other again after that kind of stupid argument is going to keep me in limbo about what life is about for a long time.

Who can I tell about this fight and why we fought and how I desperately want to call him back. How I want him to wait for me so that I can die in the crash with him.

In my head, all night long, ever since Eileen

came up to my room to tell me what happened, I have played that fight over in my head. I'm looking for that hole in it where I can crawl in and become a part of the newsreel rather than someone watching it.

I have no other options. Either we finish that fight or I go with him in the car.

I'll never see him again. He's never coming back ever. We should be at his apartment right now, asleep, next to each other with our whole lives ahead of us.

Yes, that is what should be happening right now.

Why did he have to go off and get killed like that? At the bottom of the hill in that stupid awful car that should have been junked months ago? Now Charles is dead and the fellow who ran into him is dead and their bodies incinerated by the fire that burst out when their cars collided.

I never said I wanted to go to Florida. He was right, who objects to going to Paris? I really thought I wanted to be where it was warm. It is so cold here. I was tired of it. I don't care about the cold anymore Charles.

I should have been more specific. I could have named an island. Then we wouldn't have fought. He wouldn't have walked away angry.

I'm angry, angrier with myself now but then...
I thought what a stupid insensitive thing to say to your future wife. When he said that he thought all

of us liked to go to Florida, I should have kept my mouth shut and let him sound stupid, like Goldie would have advised.

Now we'll never talk about this. He'll never curl up with me and apologize for hurting me.

Then I can remind him that I didn't like being lumped in with all those people in Skokie who flock to Miami in the winter. Didn't he know how hard I worked not to be that girl from Skokie?

I asked him how he could be so nice and kind and sensitive one minute and such an asshole the next, he looked at me and said that it just came naturally and walked out of my room. He told me to be ready in an hour. He would be back to pick me up for dinner. If I was lucky.

I guess my luck ran out.

He's not 10 hours late; he's dead. I want that argument to be finished and resolved. It can't end now because Charles isn't here to finish it. I was ready for him to pick me up and for us to say none of that mattered.

Charles didn't walk into my room, it was Eileen who appeared with this horrible look on her face. I was ready for a fight with Charles. Looking at her face, the fight fizzled out of me. I thought something horrible had happened to her. Like magic the anger disappeared and in its place was my concern for her.

I even thought that the president had been

assassinated. But then I wondered who would shoot Nixon? I wasn't really listening to the words Eileen said. I had no idea why she took me in her arms. I never liked Nixon and neither did she.

Then I heard her say Charles.

"What happened to Charles?" I asked her and pushed her away from me. I didn't mean to be mean but I was so confused.

From that stupid fight to him being unrecognizably dead in about 10 minutes time.

It's 4:00 am and about 11 hours ago he was supposed to pick me up and take me to Tony's house for dinner.

Did he do that on purpose? Did he race in front of that car so he could show that guy how his car wasn't a piece of shit? That it was just as good as Charles wanted it to be? That no one got in the way of Charles Foster Payne?

Losing Charles so fast, so soon and so stupidly with that fight unfinished inside me—damn it. That beautiful body is all burned up. Let me finish with him the right way, end it the right way. Not like this.

Charles is dead. I have nothing more to say.

Charles' family held a memorial service for Charles in the church in Town. We all sat still and rigid with the grief. It is still unbelievable that he is gone. Friends and his family filled the place up so that there were no empty seats. We all loved him so much.

It was a beautiful service. His brothers spoke, there are three of them. They all referred to him as the crazy guy in their family who never did what was expected of him. They had always for-given him because he was so lovable and loving and never meant anyone any harm.

His father tried to speak but he looked like he had been run over by a truck.

One of Charles' sisters (he had two sisters) mentioned that Charles had been engaged to me. I never knew he had such a large family.

The whole family treated me well. It was spooky to see his family gathered together for the first time and not for him to be with us. However, it was even spookier that they all looked like him except for their father. He seems to have grown out of a different stock and that he might die of grief any minute. Charles' mother looked like she was in charge. She had that strong jaw like Charles'. I imagine it was his mother who put this service together so quickly.

When I walked into the church, I saw his coffin at the front. The coffin was closed, covered in a white cloth and covered with flowers, so many flowers I wondered how they stayed on the coffin. The whole place smelled like a hot house because of them.

We had driven to the church, Lauren took me, in a blizzard. They were predicting so much of snow that everyone was going to the service and then getting out of town as soon as they could. Mrs. Payne had worried about all these details, I thought, and none of us can remain to show Charles the respect he deserves.

There was nothing religious in the service at all. I thought there might be a priest to read a passage from the Bible or to say a word about the meaning of Charles's life and now the loss of it. The church itself had been stripped of anything religious. In the sparseness of the moment, perhaps that was the best plan.

Flowers and candles were all that Charles needed to be remembered by or with.

Tony sat on one side of me and Lauren on the other. Each held my hand but with a different purpose. Lauren helped me get through this one awful moment. Tony was there to remind me of all that the three of us had done together.

I've never been to a funeral for someone my own age before. Looking at his coffin and thinking that so little of his physical being existed anymore, it wasn't possible to equate the man I had inside my head with the box in the church. The box became the end of the road. I don't even know how to talk about death or what it feels like to lose someone like him.

I still wear the engagement ring. I can't take it off because now it feels like a part of me.

I sat and stared at the coffin until they took it out of the church and placed it in a hearse that was going to take it/him back to New York.

That box was haunting and I wanted to throw myself on it so that they could burn it and me together. It was the pressure of Lauren's hand on me that kept me in my seat. I think if she hadn't been there next to me, I would have become quite the mental patient for all of them them to see. I would have done my Pops one better.

I think too, I didn't want to spoil Charles' memory by acting like that. He would have had a fit if he knew I behaved like that at his funeral.

I wisely kept my mouth shut that I was the cause of Charles' death. That wasn't the best moment to tell them.

After the service, Mrs. Payne asked Tony and me to join them for lunch. Tony went with them but I told her I couldn't. I couldn't. I couldn't sit down with them to eat. I don't eat now. I can't put anything inside me. I'm blocked up. Nothing goes in and nothing comes out. A perfect homeostasis.

Because I couldn't join them for lunch, she

took me aside to talk. She held both my hands in her gloved ones. Mine had no gloves and were cold; even in her gloves, her hands were cold too. We looked at each other, the two most important women in Charles' life before his death.

Her resemblance to him was even more striking when we stood so close to each other. I also noticed that like Charles, it took her time to speak. Like him, she had to find the precise words she wanted to use.

"I have something for you. It isn't much but it is what I think Charles would have wanted me to do for you. Any time you ever need anything, please, Scags, come to me. As you know, Charles didn't talk much. He was a lot like me, I'm afraid. But he had the most beautiful things to say about you. He loved you and so do I."

She put an envelope in my hands and closed them. She walked back to her family, all of whom waited on her and then walked out of the church together. They took Charles with them.

I shoved the envelope into my pocket. Lauren had been waiting for Mrs. Payne to finish talking to me and arrived at my side to help me out the door and to her car.

As we walked out of the church, I said good bye to as many people as I could. No one wanted to hang out. How fitting I thought that Charles' funeral was on the day of the first blizzard. I didn't even know if he liked snow.

The snow was deep and Lauren had to park quite a ways down the road. There had been so many cars for the funeral. Walking in the snow was hard work. I concentrated my whole mind on getting to the car without falling.

Just as I approached the car, someone grabbed me. I may have yelled because I remember Lauren's shocked face turning to see what had happened. It was Prof. Keating who grabbed me and then he needed to help keep me from falling. He was the last person I wanted to see.

He looked like he hadn't slept in a long time but I didn't care.

"I know I shouldn't be bothering you right now," he said, "but I wanted you to know how sorry I am that Charles is gone."

"Thank you," I said and turned away.

"Wait," he called at me.

I stopped but I didn't turn again to look at him. His breath filled up the air around me as he said, "We're leaving here. My whole family hates living in the country so we are going back to the city. I wanted you to know that."

I kept still, waiting for him to say good bye. And I waited and waited until Lauren came back to get me. She asked me why I was standing there. Why didn't I get into the car already?

I did get into the car already but not before I

turned to look back. Prof. Keating was running to catch up with his family. I got into the car and we waited for the heater to warm us up. It took Lauren's car a while to warm up and melt the snow. Then she got out of the car again to clear the windshield.

She pulled into the road and drove slowly towards the College. At the entrance to the College, I made her stop. It wasn't smart to stop the car in the midst of the blizzard right in the middle of the highway. She knew why I needed to do this and we both got out of the car and stood side by side with the engine running where Charles had made his fatal choice.

How many times had I been a passenger in that car? How many times had I seen him gun the engine in order to beat the car coming at him? But that day when he gunned his engine, it choked, and stalled and he and the other guy died. In a huge burst of flames, the two of them were incinerated. There was no way to identify either of them.

I have no idea what was put into that coffin or what would be buried. But it wasn't my Charles. Not the one I loved.

Lauren stood quietly beside me and held my hand. She didn't say a word or try to make it seem like things would be okay.

She is the friend I have always wanted.

I'm on the train returning to Skokie and will be home before Christmas. The train is very full with people ready to be festive for the holidays. Many colored packages fill the overhead bins. Presents galore.

I don't feel like partying. It's still impossible to believe that one week ago Charles died. I called Mama to tell her to pick me up at the station as we planned when I left in September. She didn't ask me about Charles or what had happened to change my plans. Someone from the College must have called her to tell her what had happened. They are like that there. So thoughtful and helpful at the worst of times without saying a word.

Mama must be wondering what shape I am in after this experience. She won't say a word until she has seen me. That's Mama.

I'm going home. What a different life I thought I had a week ago. In my head, I had begun writing post cards to friends and family from the places Charles and I traveled to. I filled each card with wonderful descriptions of all the things we saw and all the new things I was now able to do.

I'll go back to the College at the end of this break. With Charles, Prof. Keating, Eileen and Philip not there, it will be a bit like starting all over again. I have something good to say about that though, I did well in all my classes, so I'll be returning knowing that I did what I set out to do.

All the other stuff was extra-curricular.

That's a pretty bloodless summation of this term: I got good grades. My boyfriend is dead. The man who wanted to be my boyfriend left. The friends who couldn't be my friends moved to Mexico.

Sometimes things aren't what they seem. If ever. Maybe I'm too young to need to be that certain of anything.

I opened the envelope Charles' mother gave me. I was alone in my room after the memorial service. Sylvie had already packed her things and gone home. She left me a wonderful card saying how much she liked being my roommate and next term she's getting an apartment off campus. She left her portion of the room clean for the first time.

I opened the envelope and found a card inside. Mrs. Payne had written a note to me in exactly the same handwriting Charles used. She told me she missed her son tremendously. She was sorry there would be no wedding. She repeated much of what she had said at the church and then said that she was giving me a check, that she hoped I wouldn't mind her doing that. It was to honor the love that Charles and I had had for each other. She knew it was priceless and that no amount of money could equal it. I looked at the amount she had written on the check and my eyes blurred over. I had never seen that amount of money made out in my name before and I doubt I ever will.

She said, she hoped it would help to make my life easier and that no one at the College needed to know. Separately, they were going to offer a scholarship in Charles's name so I wasn't to do anything foolish but to have an easier life.

She signed it in an odd way, I never would have thought she would do this. She wrote:

Love from Charles' mother

Tony dropped by to say good bye to me as I cleaned up the room. He looked gloomy too. He gave me a big hug. He said he would be back in February and look out for me as Charles would have wanted him to do. I told him I would look out for him too as Charles always wanted his friends to be friends.

When Tony walked out the door, I had that vision of Charles leaving again. I fell down on the bed and into a deep sleep for several hours.

Alex woke me up. He too wanted to say good bye. He had hoped we could go for a run but the weather wasn't good for that.

We stood at the window in my room. Somehow being with Alex is always about being in the outdoors even when you can't be. The untouched white snow below us held the sun's glare in such a way that it looked like a huge crystal cloth covered the earth.

"I'll be back in February," I told him."

"I had no doubts that you'd be back. I want you on my team."

I agreed and we held onto each other for a long time. Before he left my room, he turned to me and said, "I owe you an apology. You did pick a good guy. He loved you and quit the drugs. I respect that, Scags. I do. I'm glad not to be losing you."

I finished packing and made sure to hide that note and check from Charles' mother.

Lauren gave herself the job of making sure I ate, had someone to talk to and hand out tissues. She also drove me to the train station and said a long good bye to me. I know when I return in February, she'll be one of the first people I go see. She invited me to come back early if I wanted to and stay with her. I really do have a good friend. I may need to take her up on that.

The food on the train is better than I remember from my ride out East. It may taste good because there isn't much to do on the train except eat. This time I'm enjoying eating in the dining car with the other passengers. I don't have to say much of anything to anyone but they give me a reason to smile.

When I can see out the window, it is snowing everywhere. Each time we stop, I pull back the curtain and in the glass the lights from the station are refracted in such a way that they look like ornaments on a Christmas tree. Everything looks so beautiful and yet I can't feel that beauty. I only know it exists.

My mind is filled going home with all the new plants that have taken root in me. I have found the means, I think, to keep sprouting.

My winter break reading list has filled up, including lots of Virginia Woolf. No writer has inspired me as she did with her wise words about being a woman and learning to write.

She's right too about time. Women haven't enjoyed enough time yet on their own to do all the things we want to do. I will become a part of that work too, I'm sure.

As to you, Charles, at least you had the good sense to give me that lock of your hair. I have had the good sense to tape it into the back of this diary. Every day I open the book at the back and stroke your hair, my Handsome Charles before I write down all the things that are happening to me.

I miss you.

Permissions

Permissions have been gratefully granted for the following material to be reproduced in part in this book:

Excerpt from "Skunk Hour" from COLLECTED POEMS by Robert Lowell © 2003 by Harriet Lowell and Sheridan Lowell. Used by permission of Farrar, Straus and Giroux, LLC

The lines from "Night in the Kitchen," Copyright © 1993 by Adrienne Rich. Copyright © 1969 by W. W. Norton & Company, Inc, from Collected Early Poems: 1950–1970 by Adrienne Rich. Used by permission of the author and W. W. Norton & Company, Inc.

The lines from Lawrence Ferlinghetti's poem "I AM WAITING." Copyright © 1958 by Lawrence Ferlinghetti. Reprinted by permission of Lawrence Ferlinghetti.

We thank The Society of Authors as the Literary Representative of the Estate of Virginia Woolf for permission to quote from "A Room of One's Own."